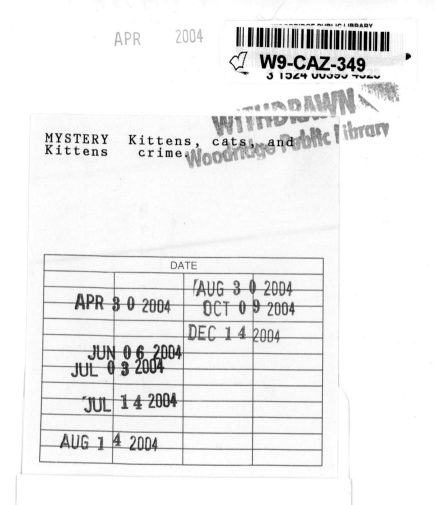

MYSTERY   Kittens, cats, and
Kittens   crime.

DATE		
		AUG 3 0 2004
APR 3 0 2004		OCT 0 9 2004
		DEC 1 4 2004
JUN 0 6 2004		
JUL 0 3 2004		
JUL 1 4 2004		
AUG 1 4 2004		

Kittens, Cats, and Crime

Kittens, Cats, and Crime

Edited by ED GORMAN

Five Star • Waterville, Maine

First Edition
First Printing: March 2003

Published in 2003 in conjunction with
Tekno Books and Ed Gorman.

Set in 11 pt. Plantin by Minnie B. Raven.

Printed in the United States on permanent paper.

Library of Congress Cataloging-in-Publication Data

Kittens, cats, and crime / edited by Ed Gorman.
        p. cm.—(Five Star first edition mystery series)
    Contents: Introduction / by John Helfers—The cat's
meow / by Christine Matthews and Robert J. Randisi—
Sardines for tea / by Lillian Stewart Carl—Cat nap /
by Kristine Kathryn Rusch—The breath of bast /
by P. N. Elrod—Cat among the rabbits / by Edward D.
Hoch—Paw-trait of a murderer / by John Helfers—
The smile of a cat / by Brendan DuBois—The Christmas
kitten / by Ed Gorman—The cat's mother /
by Mat Coward—In the lowlands / by Gary A. Braunbeck
—Hell matter / by Jean Rabe.
    ISBN 0-7862-5032-1 (hc : alk. paper)
    1. Cats—Fiction.   2. Detective and mystery stories,
American.   I. Gorman, Edward.   II. Series.
PS648.C38K58 2003
  813'.087203629752—dc21   2002192829

Table of Contents

Introduction

John Helfers

In *The Fine Art of Murder*, the seminal book on the mystery genre, author Lawrence Block came up with a delightful idea for categorizing mystery novels: those with cats, and those without cats.

Although this notion should at least elicit a smile from readers, upon looking more closely it's probably not as humorous an idea as it first sounds (I'm sure Larry wrote the article as humor, but with him, one never knows . . .). After all, there are many, many authors who have had success in the mystery field publishing so-called cat mysteries. Lilian Jackson Braun. Rita Mae Brown. Carole Nelson Douglas. The list goes on. And anthologies featuring cat mysteries? More than you could shake a stick at. Besides the excellent *Cat Crimes* series, there have been many other collections of feline detectives and four-footed sleuths published over the years. The fact is that cats and mystery go together like ice cream and hot fudge.

The reasons for this have never really been explained. One theory is that cats themselves possess such an intrinsic mystique that it just makes perfect sense to place them in a mystery setting. With their imperious, all-knowing gaze, one would certainly think that if they ever deigned to put their feline minds to it, they could solve any crime they wanted (although the actions of the two cats I live with certainly prove the exception to this theory). Whatever the reason is, the reality in the mystery field is that cats and crime are a very popular combination, and the pairing shows no sign of waning any time soon.

With that in mind, we are pleased to present this collection of cat mysteries, the second in our series (after the well-received *Felonious Felines*) of cat mystery anthologies. In here you will find both modern and historical stories by some of the best writers in the business. From P. N. Elrod's period piece about a delivery man who finds more than he bargains for to Brendan DuBois's modern dark tale about a would-be criminal who gets his come-uppance at the claws of a cat, here are eleven stories featuring everybody's (well, almost everybody's) favorite animal detectives.

The Cat's Meow

A Gil & Claire Hunt story

Christine Matthews and Robert J. Randisi

"There, did you hear it that time?" Claire whispered.

Gil laid with his back to her. "No. I didn't hear anything," he groaned.

"Come on." She gently yanked at his arm. "If you kneel on the pillows and put your ear against the wall . . ."

"Go . . . to . . . sleep. . . ."

"Just get up . . ."

"Please. I'm exhausted," he begged, still not rolling over to face her in the darkness.

Claire got out of bed and checked the clock glowing on her night table. "It's three o'clock in the morning. How can you not hear that wailing? How can everyone just . . . sleep?" She grabbed her robe and marched out of the room.

Walking into the living room, she switched on the lamp next to the sofa. Then she stood in the middle of the large room and listened intently, trying not to make any movement or sound that would interfere with her concentration.

There! A low, frightening moan. It sounded like it was coming from the condo next to theirs.

She went to the front door and slowly opened it, peeking into the quiet hallway. Gil and Claire Hunt were the newest residents in the high rise building on Brentwood Avenue. They'd owned their condo for almost five years. The other residents had been there for much longer; some had leases dating to the ground-breaking ceremony almost forty years ago . . . at least, that's what the doorman, Harry Wales, had told her once.

Tip-toeing into the carpeted hallway, Claire gently pulled her front door closed behind her. The oblong hall had recently been covered with metallic wallpaper. The soft taupe background made the small patterns of pink, white and green leaves stand out. The thick green carpeting felt good as her bare feet sunk into the deep pile. And the brand new chandelier bolted to the middle of the ceiling dazzled, illuminating the area brightly.

There were four condos on their floor. She slowly walked to the door of the unit next to theirs. A common wall stretched the length of their living rooms, bathrooms and master bedrooms. She stood away from the front door, not wanting to be spotted through the peephole she knew was standard in each door.

As she pressed her ear against the wall the metallic leaves felt cool against her cheek. The quiet in the hallway was like a thick blanket inside her head.

When she was satisfied that there was nothing moving around inside her neighbor's living room she hurried back to her own front door, pushed it open and rushed inside.

"So?" Gil asked as they sat across from each other the next morning at breakfast.

"What?" Claire put her knife down.

"We've discussed what to do on your day off. Decided on English muffins over bagels. Read the mail and even figured out what we're going to do for dinner."

"What's your point?" She stared at him, knowing full well what he was getting at.

He wiped his lips with a napkin. "Tell me, did you find out where your imaginary noise was coming from?"

"Well, no . . ."

"Can't you even admit that it could have been a dream?"

"No, I was awake."

"Or a ghost? Remember how you got when you heard that this condo might be haunted?" He grinned at her and as much as she loved him—or maybe because of it—she wanted to scream until he took her seriously.

"Don't get started on that again. This was not a ghost—it was real. Kind of a low, whining sob. It sounded like something in pain . . . crying." She shivered. "An animal—like a cat."

"Oh, well, if it's only a cat—"

"We've lived here almost five years and never heard a sound like that before. Aren't you even a little bit curious? And how can you say 'only' a cat?"

Gil stood up and pulled the curtains behind him aside. Two large sliding glass doors revealed a panoramic view of the city of Clayton, Missouri. An early morning dusting of snow had covered the streets, causing traffic to creep along. "Honey, we live in a congested area of town, on the corner of a busy intersection. There's all kinds of noises out there. Day and night."

"Why are you being so bull-headed about this?" Claire asked her husband. "The sound wasn't outside, it was near us, in the building. It felt like it was right under our bed."

He knew when she was like this he wouldn't get any peace. It wasn't that his wife was obsessive, just . . . single-minded.

"Okay, Claire, what do you want me to do? Go door to door? Ask everyone in the building if they heard anything last night?"

She walked into the living room, her hands buried deep in the pockets of her fleece robe. "I was thinking about that and I got so depressed."

He came up behind her and wrapped his arms around her.

"Now why would you get so upset about this? I bet tonight you won't hear a thing."

"It's not that. I got depressed when I realized we don't know one single person in this place. It makes me feel so isolated. When I was a kid, my family knew everybody on the whole block."

He led her to the sofa and they sat down together.

"Honey, there are more than thirty condo units in the building. How can you possibly—"

"I don't expect to know everyone, but we aren't even friendly with the people on this floor and there's only three of them. Three, Gil. Is that too much to expect from us?"

Gil sat back and thought a moment. "Directly across from us is Irene, or is her name Colleen? You know, the one with the dog. Smoker Lady is next to her. And next to us is Stereo Guy."

Claire looked over toward her husband. "How can you think just because we've nicknamed our neighbors by their most obvious characteristics that we know them? And I'm almost positive her name's Irene."

"Charlie," he said.

"What?"

"The dog's name is Charlie."

Claire stood up. "I'm getting dressed. It's obvious we're not going to have any kind of serious conversation right now."

Gil chased after her down the hall. "Hey, does this mean you're not going to take me out to lunch today?"

"Go to your bookstore and leave me alone."

"What fun would that be?"

When Gil came to bed that evening he found Claire huddled on her side, reading the paperback she'd bought earlier that day.

"Since when did you start reading self-help books?" he asked as he crawled over to her.

"It's comforting."

He studied her profile, wondering what he could say to cheer her up.

Absent-mindedly she stroked his hair while she continued reading.

"Claire, sweetheart, can you put the book down for a minute?"

"Why?"

"So I can tell you that you're not a terrible person just because you don't know your neighbors on a first name basis."

She slipped a bookmark into the paperback and laid it beside her. Turning to face him she smiled. "I know I'm not terrible. But thanks for saying it anyway. It's just that sometimes . . ."

Before she could finish her sentence an ear-piercing wail filled the room.

Gil cleared the bed. "What the hell was that?"

"It wasn't that loud last night." Claire got out of bed.

"You mean I slept through something like that last night?" Gil looked at his wife, amazed.

"Yep." She pulled a white sweater over her nightgown. "Put on your pants."

"Why?" he asked, stepping into his jeans.

"Because we're going to find out where that's coming from."

"Now?" He checked the clock radio. "But it's ten thirty."

"I hear people banging their doors in this building at all hours. Besides, ten thirty isn't that late." Claire tucked the hem of her gown into a pair of brown slacks. Then slipping her feet into blue fuzzy slippers she said, "Come on."

They tried the condo across the hall first. A dog started barking as soon as they knocked.

Gil asked Irene if she had heard a cat in the building lately.

"A cat?" she asked, screwing her face into a frown so that it had even more lines than usual. She was either a hard-lived fifty or a good seventy. "I think if we'd heard a cat Charlie would have acted up. Wouldn't you, boy?" She patted her dog affectionately on the head.

Charlie didn't look up at his mistress; he was too intent on trying to lick Gil's hand. Gil kept flicking his fingers to dissuade the animal, but it wasn't working. Finally he stuck both hands in his pockets.

"No," Irene said, "no cat. Why?"

"We just thought we heard something the last few nights, meowing over and over," Claire told her.

"I sleep like the dead, so I doubt if I would've heard it," the older woman said. "Charlie sleeps real good, too. I think his hearing's going on him, though."

Gil backed up, trying to get away from Charlie's prying nose and the dog started to follow.

"Charlie! Stay!" Irene snapped. "I don't let him out in the hall without me."

"Well, we'll keep looking," Gil said. "Thanks, Irene."

"Sure, Gil, and . . . uh . . . ." She stared questioningly at Claire.

"Claire."

"Oh yes, of course. Well . . . bye, you two."

"See?" Claire hissed to the closed door.

"What?"

"It's like I'm invisible. She knows your name, but not mine. How come?"

"I don't know, sweetie," he said. "Maybe I just run into her more often than you do. Like when I get the mail."

"And the doorman."

"What about him?"

"The doorman . . . whatsisname?"

"Harry?"

"Yes," she said, "he knows your name, too, and not mine."

"Sweetie," Gil pointed out, "you don't know his name."

"That's beside the point," she grumbled.

When Smoker Lady opened her door they were hit in the face with a blast of stale, warm air. In her late sixties she'd already been in the hospital once for heart surgery, but it hadn't even slowed down her smoking in the slightest.

"Cat?" she asked, pulling her faded housecoat closer around her. "Why would there be a cat in here? Who has a cat? Bad enough Irene's got that dog, although as dogs go he's okay, I guess, but let me tell you about cats. They're no good. Not a loyal bone in their sneaky little bodies, and they hiss at ya all the time." Behind her the TV droned on.

"Well, okay—" Gil said.

"And they should be declawed," she went on. "They scratch ya for no reason at all—"

"We just wanted to know if you'd heard a cat," Claire said, in a rush.

"A cat? I haven't heard a cat. That's why I got a unit on

15

a higher floor, so I wouldn't be hearing every damn cat, dog and kid. Kids, now lemme tell ya about kids—"

"Thanks, very much," Claire said, and backed away, tugging at Gil's sleeve. The woman, seeing that she had lost her audience, closed her door, trapping most of the smoke back inside, but letting a small cloud drift to the ceiling of the hall.

"She didn't seem to know either of our names," Gil said. "And thank God!"

Stereo Guy was the newest tenant to the floor, other than the Hunts. He was so named because frequently a carton would appear outside his door, delivered by mail or UPS, which was marked as stereo equipment. When his surround sound speakers arrived Gil and Claire were expecting to be blasted off the floor, but so far the walls seemed able to handle it all.

They rang his bell and got no reply.

"Not home," Gil said.

"Have you ever managed to figure out his schedule?"

"No, Watson, but then I haven't really tried."

"I don't see him when I leave in the morning." Claire left at dawn to host her morning show on the Home Shopping Mall.

"I don't see him, either." Gil left at a more reasonable hour to open his University City bookstore.

They returned to their own condo and closed the door.

"Are you going to the studio tomorrow?" Gil asked.

"Yes," she said. "I'm not on the air but I'm shooting some promos and voice-overs."

"Well, you can try our neighbor in the morning, then."

She stared at him. "Alone? I'm not going to talk to him alone."

Gil pulled the covers up to his chin. "Wake me before you take your shower. I just need enough time to get dressed and have a cup of coffee."

She kissed him quickly on the cheek. "I love you, Gil."

At eight a.m. the next morning they were at Stereo Guy's door again, ringing the bell. There was no answer. During the night they had each heard the cat's meow again but remained in bed, determined to start the morning by finding out where the noise was coming from.

"Still not home," Claire complained, "and I can't wait around. I have to go to work."

"I'll ride down in the elevator with you," Gil said. "Maybe Harry can tell me something about Stereo Guy."

"Great idea," she said. "More and more you prove to me that you're not just another pretty face."

Gil saw Claire off, watching her drive out of the parking garage beneath the building. Then he took the elevator back to the lobby.

"Hey, Mr. Hunt," the doorman said. "What's shaking?"

"Not much, Harry. Listen, do you happen to know if anyone on my floor has a cat?"

"On *your* floor? Nope. I know Mrs. Moxley has a dog."

"That's Irene, right?"

"Yes, sir."

"Anybody in the building have a cat?"

"Not that I know of. Why? Have you seen one?"

"No," Gil said. "We've been hearing something wailing the last few nights. A godawful noise."

Harry thought for a moment. "No, as far as I know there're no cats in the entire building. But I'll be sure to let you know if I see one."

17

"Okay then, thanks, Harry," Gil said. As he started for the door he remembered Stereo Guy. "Ah, Harry, do you know anything about the man in the condo next to ours?"

"Mr. Walthers?"

"I don't know his name," Gil explained. "All I know is he gets a lot of stereo equipment delivered."

"That's him," Harry said. "Moved in just before you did, if I remember right. He used to work for some recording studio on the coast. Hey, maybe that's it, Mr. Hunt. You know, some people play the damnedest things on tape. Maybe that's where your cat sounds are coming from."

"At three in the morning?" Gil shook his head. "I don't think so. Besides, every time we ring his bell he's not home."

"Well, if you think something's wrong I could get my key—"

"No, no," Gil said, "I don't think there's any reason for that."

"Well," Harry said, "if you decide you need some help, Mr. H, just let me know."

That evening, as they sat down to dinner, the couple discussed their day. The matter of the wailing cat had been forgotten while they caught up on each other's news. As Gil brought a forkful of chicken to his mouth the phone rang.

"Damn telemarketers," he grumbled. "Why do they always call at dinnertime?"

"Just ignore it," she said. "The machine will—"

"Mr. H? Are you there?" They recognized Harry's voice coming from the answering machine. "I found out something about that cat of yours."

Before Gil could say a word Claire raced for the phone.

"Harry, this is Mrs. Hunt. What did you find out?"

"The night man, Bob, I don't know if you've met him, he hasn't been here that long—"

"I don't think I have." Claire tried hurrying the conversation along. "What did Bob tell you?"

"In the condo directly above you there're these new tenants. Real nice folks, young couple, he says, but Bob's in his late sixties. Anyway, says the guy is a musician. Plays second violin at Powell Hall. There was an article in *The Riverfront Times* about him moving here from Kansas City."

"And, these people own a cat?" she asked, impatiently.

"So, Bob said he saw the wife carrying one of those pet carriers the day they moved in. I'm surprised you haven't heard them walking around up there."

"I am, too," Claire said.

"Well, Mrs. Hunt, I guess that clears up your mystery. You're probably either hearing their cat, or his violin. Tell Mr. H if there's anything else I can do—"

"I'll tell him, Harry. Thanks."

"We have new neighbors?" Gil asked, after swallowing the last of his potato.

Claire put her hand on her hip and nodded. "I haven't heard them walking around, have you?"

"No," he said, "but then we're at work during the day."

"Harry says we're hearing their cat, or his violin."

"Well, he'd be a little odd and very insensitive if he was playing his violin at three a.m., but the cat we can believe, right?"

"Hmm," Claire said.

"What?"

"Why don't we hear them walking around?" she asked. "We used to hear those other people . . . what was their name?"

"The Corbetts."

"Right," she said.

"They had two kids," he pointed out. "We heard them all the time."

Gil got up, moved around behind his wife and put his hands on her shoulders.

"Sweetie," he said, "we found the cat. Let's be happy with that."

"Hmm," she said, again.

It was two thirty-four a.m. when Claire was awakened. As she squinted to look at her husband laying next to her in the darkness he startled her by speaking.

"Yes, I heard it. And it sure as hell wasn't a violin. And if it was—I think we have to talk to our new neighbor about the lack of consideration regarding other people's sleep."

Claire was slipping into her robe by the time Gil came around to her side of the bed.

"Where are you going?" he asked, trailing after her as she rushed toward the kitchen.

"To find that bottle of Merlot we bought last week."

Gil watched as his wife dragged a chair across the kitchen floor and then climbed on the seat. He held the back of the chair, steadying it as Claire arched on her toes to see the back of the top shelf. "Honey, are you okay?"

When Claire didn't answer he asked, "Claire, can you hear me?" Touching her leg gently he leaned in closer. "Are you asleep? Claire, answer me—give me a sign that you're conscious."

"Ahh, here it is. I knew it was back behind the brandy." She jumped down onto the floor. Looking at her husband she saw the concern in his eyes. "Gil, sweetie, I'm fine. I just want to have something to take to our new neighbors."

"Why would you want to . . ."

"Because, I'm trying to learn from my mistakes. I want to know the people who live so close to us . . . and I want them to know me. How can I complain about how impersonal everything's become when I don't try to break through the boundaries. It's time I started—"

"You want to use this bottle of Merlot to get invited into their apartment, don't you?"

"Exactly," she said. "Once inside we can see if they have a cat . . . but we can also get to know them a little."

"Tomorrow," he said, taking the bottle from her. "Start implementing your plan tomorrow. I don't think anyone would appreciate a visit from the Welcome Wagon at this hour."

"You were always the wise one," she said. "But I do feel better just having a plan."

"So do I. Maybe we'll finally locate the source of that horrible noise. Where are you going now?"

"I'm exhausted," she said, hurrying down the hall. "Aren't you coming to bed?"

The next day Claire came home as soon as her morning show was finished, pleading a migraine. Gil stayed home to wait for her and had his assistant open the bookstore for him. It was unusual for both of them to be home at one in the afternoon, and as Claire was wrapping the bottle of Merlot in silver paper she found left over from Christmas they both heard sounds from upstairs.

"What's that?" Claire asked.

"Walking," he said. "She's walking around."

They listened intently and then Claire said, "It sounds like somebody's . . . pacing."

And then they heard the other sound.

"Is that . . . a cat?" Claire asked.

Gil looked at her. "There's only one way to find out."

They had to ring the doorbell twice before the door was opened by a fairly attractive blonde in her early thirties. She was breathing quickly and looked a bit harried.

"Can I help you?" she asked.

"We're your neighbors from downstairs," Claire said. "I'm Claire Hunt and this is my husband, Gil."

"Oh, well . . . how do you do?"

"We just wanted to welcome you to the building," Claire said, trying to get a look past the woman into the apartment.

The woman seemed undecided about how to act, which struck both Gil and Claire as odd.

"I'm Cindy," she said, finally. "My husband is Benny. He—he's not home, right now . . . but why don't you come on in?"

"Thank you," Claire said.

The woman backed up to allow them to enter, then closed the door behind them. When she turned, Claire held out the bottle of Merlot.

"Welcome, neighbor."

"Thank you." She pulled at the string Claire had tied at the top and unwrapped the bottle. "Why don't we have some now?" She turned to Gil. "Mr. Hunt, would you do the honors?"

"Of course."

"There's a corkscrew in the kitchen."

He nodded and headed for the kitchen, the layout of this unit being the same as their own.

"I'm sorry for the mess," Cindy said to Claire. "I can't seem to get my act together."

"That's all right," Claire said, although there really didn't seem to be much mess, to her. There were no boxes, and just a few newspapers on a chair or two. There was, however, something in the air—a scent—that was tickling at Claire's memory.

"Please, sit down," Cindy said, moving some of the papers.

Claire sat in one of the armchairs while Cindy sat on the sofa. The furnishings were clean, functional, not expensive at all. From the kitchen she could hear Gil opening drawers, looking for the corkscrew.

Suddenly, Claire realized Cindy was staring at her.

"I'm sorry," the other woman said, "but you look so familiar to me."

"I'm a host on the Home Shopping Mall. I don't know if you get it—"

"Of course! Claire Hunt! Oh my God, I love your show! See that lamp there?" Cindy pointed to a large brass lamp on an end table, which Claire recognized. "And these tennis shoes?" She proudly pointed to her feet. "All from your shopping channel. I love your stuff."

"Well, thank you."

They both heard a drawer in the kitchen open and Cindy called out, "Did you find it?"

Gil came out of the kitchen holding the bottle in one hand and the corkscrew in the other. "I found it." There was a triumphant look in his eyes that Claire thought might have to do with something other than a corkscrew. "Now all we need are glasses."

Two glasses of wine each later she was showing them to the door when Gil stepped on something. He looked down and saw that it was a rubber toy. He bent down and picked it up, barely had time to see exactly what it was when Cindy plucked it from his hand.

"That's, uh, Baby's."

"Baby?" he asked.

"Our cat."

It was the first time any of them had approached the subject.

"Ah," he said, looking at Claire. "We've been wondering who had a cat."

"Oh . . . can you hear him?"

"Sometimes," Claire said, "at night, when he . . . wails?"

Cindy blinked. "Well, he does do that sometimes. I'll try to keep him quiet from now on."

"Oh, that's okay," Claire said. "I mean, we *hardly* hear him at all."

"A baby," Gil said, when they got back to their own apartment. "Not a violin, not a cat. A baby."

"I know."

Gil stared at her.

"How do you know?"

"First tell me how you know?"

"The kitchen," he said. "In going through the drawers I found some plastic baby bottles, and rubber nipples."

"I smelled it."

"What?"

"I knew I smelled something when we walked in," Claire said.

"A baby? You could smell a baby?"

"Babies smell very special, plus there's other smells— powder, wipes, poop, spit up—"

"Please," he said, holding up his hands, "I remember from my own kids."

"Well, so did I, that's how I knew. Also, did you see any sign of a cat? I mean, was there a food dish in the kitchen? Toys? Did you see any cat hair?"

"No," he said, "none of that."

"So that's the wailing we hear at night," she said. "It's the baby. Why would they want to keep a baby a secret? There's no rule against babies here."

"She looked kind of . . . spooked when she opened the door at first, and she was real tentative about inviting us in . . . but if she was trying to hide it why give me the run of the kitchen?"

"Maybe that was a mistake."

Gil scratched his head. "Maybe we're blowing this out of proportion. So we don't hear them walking around in the evenings. So what? Maybe they're just considerate and they don't walk with the baby in the evenings."

"Baby's have to be walked all the time, Gil, especially when they cry. Their master bedroom would be above ours," Claire said. "The baby's room is the other bedroom. Maybe she walks him at night in there and we don't hear it."

"But we hear it cry?"

"The walls here are well insulated. If they'd moved in across the hall or next door we might not have heard it, but because they live above us we do."

Gil scratched his head again. "I don't get it. Why advertise that you have a cat, but try to hide the fact that you have a baby?"

"So that when the baby cries," she guessed, "they can make people think it's a cat."

"Which means they don't want people to know they have a baby."

"But why?" she asked.

25

Gil shook his head. "We're back to square one. It doesn't make sense."

"I'm going to start dinner."

"This early?"

"Drinking in the afternoon makes me hungry."

"I thought two glasses of wine made you amorous."

She smiled at him and said, "That's in the evenings, sweetie."

Over the next few days they didn't hear the wailing, and assumed the upstairs couple had taken steps to keep the baby—or their "cat"—quiet. Although they discussed the situation a few more times, neither of them was able to come up with a solution. Gil did mention calling the police. In the end, though, they decided that they really had nothing to report that could be investigated, beyond their suspicions that the people upstairs had a baby, and didn't want anyone to know. No matter how they looked at it, that was not a crime.

On the fourth day after they had gotten a look inside the upstairs apartment, Gil received a shipment of books at his store which he'd ordered from a dealer in Kansas City. As he unpacked the books he removed the crumpled pages of the *Kansas City Star* that had been used for padding. Part of the fun of unpacking boxes from other states was taking a look at their newspapers, mostly the sports pages. This time, however, it was a page five story that caught his eye. He read it, then read it again excitedly. After he'd read it a third time he picked up the phone and called the dealer in K.C. . . .

Gil waited impatiently for Claire to get home from work. Finally, when she walked in the door he rushed to her, kissed her and said, "Read this," thrusting the newspaper into her hands.

"Is that any way to greet your wife after a hard day's—what—"

She'd glanced at the newspaper while speaking and when she spotted the story she stopped short to read it. Gil gave her time to let it all sink in.

"Where did you get this?"

"A shipment of books I got today," he said. "What do you think?"

She looked at it again, read the large type headline out loud: STILL NO SIGN OF MISSING BABY. The story went on to describe how a newborn baby had gone missing from an "area" hospital. After hours of searching the police came to the conclusion that the infant had been stolen.

"My God," Claire said. "What's the date on this?"

"Three weeks ago," Gil said, as she started to look for it.

"Okay, so we're thinking the same thing?"

"We are."

"But . . . Gil, do you know if this baby is still missing?"

"I called the dealer in Kansas City and asked," Gil said. "He said it was a big story there and he'd been following it. The baby is still missing and—get this—the police now suspect a nurse who worked at the hospital in the maternity ward. She and her husband are also missing."

Claire sat down on the sofa and Gil sat next to her.

"What do we do?" she asked. "I mean . . . this could be a coincidence."

"Honey," he said, "the people upstairs have a baby and are trying to hide that fact. Plus, when I came in tonight I asked Harry exactly when they had moved in here. He checked for me. They moved in a week after the baby went missing."

"Could they have found a place to live here in town so fast?"

"If they'd planned it, yes."

They fell silent for a few moments and then Claire said, "What if we're wrong?"

"Then we'll be embarrassed."

"Embarrassed?" she asked. "I would be mortified. We'd never be able to talk to the people upstairs again, or to Harry. My God, the word would get around, we'd probably have to leave the building . . ."

"Sweetie," he said, taking her hand. "We both have kids. What if one of ours had been stolen from the hospital? How would we have felt if someone could have helped, but didn't want to risk being embarrassed?"

Claire took a deep breath, squeezed his hand and asked, "Who do we call?"

Three days later the newspaper was on the table between them while they had their muffins and coffee. The headline said: STOLEN BABY FOUND IN CLAYTON CONDO.

"Without us they would never have known that nurse and her husband had stolen the infant and moved here with him," Claire said. She was miffed the story hadn't mentioned them.

"Lucky for the kid's parents we heard those noises coming from upstairs," Gil said.

"*We* heard?" she asked. "If I remember correctly I had to beg you to listen—"

"Okay, okay," Gil said, "you heard it first. But you know, even though we found out they had a baby up there—and he's back safe and sound with his mother and father—I still think it sounded more like a cat."

"But we know now there was no cat," Claire pointed out.

Claire picked up the paper, looked at the story and then said, "Hmph. Says the detectives were notified by a reliable source. Is that what we are now? 'Reliable'?"

"Hey," he said, picking up their dishes and cups and taking them to the sink, "I like it that way. I don't want our names in the paper in connection to this, do you?"

"Well . . . we are sort of heroes, aren't we?"

He smiled, leaned over and kissed her neck. "You've always been my hero, my love."

They were leaving for work together that day, an unusual occurrence. As they were walking to the elevator something else unusual happened. Stereo Guy's door opened and he stepped out. He was in his forties, tall and gangly; neither of them was sure they would have recognized him if he hadn't been coming out of that apartment.

"Oh," he said, startled, " 'morning."

"Good morning," Gil said. Funny, they'd spent days looking for him and now they had nothing more to say.

Suddenly, as the man started to close his door a gray cat, little more than a kitten, darted into the hall. The man reached down and caught him before he could get much further, and shoved him inside. He closed his door, locking the cat in.

"So you're the one with the cat!" Claire said, triumphantly.

"Oh, yeah," the man said. "Had him about a month. I hope he didn't keep you awake wailing in the middle of the night. I only just got him to stop doing it."

The man said good-morning again and trotted to the open elevator before the doors could close. He looked at them expectantly, silently asking if they wanted him to hold the door.

"Go ahead," Gil said. "We forgot something."

He shrugged and the doors closed. Gil and Claire stared at each other with their mouths open.

"God," she said, finally, "if his cat hadn't been wailing, or if *he* had been home, we never would have gone upstairs."

"And that baby never would have been found."

"It's weird the way things happen, sometimes," she said.

Gil was about to answer when suddenly the cat scratched at the door and they heard its plaintive, "meow!"

Sardines for Tea

Lillian Stewart Carl

I'm here to tell you, all a fellow really needs for a full life is regular meals, a place on the hearth rug, and the occasional scratch behind the ears. If the cook finds it in her heart and menu to dispense a few sardines come tea time, then that simply crosses the t's in contentment.

So imagine my disgust one afternoon when I was awakened from the all-too-rare sunbath by a caterwauling of human voices. I sat up, stretched, smoothed my whiskers, and cantered off toward the main staircase. My elder colleague, Jasper, was already poised behind the balusters, tail wrapped tidily around his forefeet, eyeing the proceedings with the air of a judge regarding the worst sort of miscreant.

"I say," said I, as I took up a position beside him, "how's a chap to get his eighteen hours of peaceful slumber when all Hades breaks loose in the entrance hall?"

"Ah, there you are, young Bingo," Jasper returned. "I regret to say that the humans have encountered a spot of bother. One moment they were sitting about in languid poses, digesting their midday repast and discussing current events. In the next moment Mrs. Arbuthnot burst through the door shrieking fit to singe one's ears. By the by," he added, "this fellow Lindbergh looks to have completed his flight, although if he wished to fly I should think a short trip amongst the trees, nabbing the odd bird on his way, would be much more sensible than this crossing the ocean business."

Nodding in agreement, I inserted my head between the balusters, all the better to see the scene below.

Even at a low volume, Mrs. Arbuthnot's voice could rattle the cups in their saucers. Now, in full cry, it made the veritable welkin ring. "Where is that constable! It's only a moment's cycle ride from the village—are you sure you rang the correct number, Violet?"

"I spoke to the man myself, Sadie, and he promised to make all possible haste." Lady Mompesson's alabaster complexion had become a shade of mauve that contrasted poorly with her gray hair.

"Constable?" I queried Jasper.

"I regret to say that Mrs. Arbuthnot has suffered a theft," he returned.

"Good heavens!"

As if to acquaint the entire household with her dilemma, Mrs. A yelled, "Stolen! The Eye of the Tiger, the Arbuthnot family heirloom! My late husband's great grandfather brought it home from India!"

"Oh, ah," said Lord Mompesson, his moustache quivering as though it had been blessed with the acute sensitivity of a cat's whiskers. "Green, was it? Whacking great emerald set in little gold doodahs?"

"I wore it last night at dinner." Mrs. A's glittering eye skewered poor Lord M like a lepidopterist a butterfly.

Celia Mompesson, slender limbs and golden curls all a-tremble, stepped forward to have a go at soothing the savage. "I'm sure it's all a misunderstanding. Perhaps you've mislaid it . . ."

"Mislaid a priceless jewel, child? I think not! I put it away in my jewelry box when I retired, and this morning before I came down for breakfast I placed the box in the wardrobe. This afternoon I found the box there but the necklace gone!"

"A bit thick, what?" I said to Jasper.

He applied a quick lick to his impeccably groomed black fur. "Positively glutinous, young Bingo."

The bulging eye of the Arbuthnot rejected Celia as small game, and turned toward the lanky form of Freddie Quirk, leaning with an unconcerned air against the library door. "You there. Quirk. Your room is next to mine. You never came down to breakfast this morning—the younger generation, lying abed til all hours—did you see or hear anything?"

Freddie stood up and straightened his tie, which was of a spiffing horseshoe design. Beside me Jasper shuddered, obviously not appreciating the man's sartorial qualities.

"Well," said Freddie, his already long face elongating to where you'd expect him to be wearing horseshoes himself, "a bit difficult, isn't it, to keep one's eyes on the next room at the same time they're closed in sleep. Although. . . ." His face corrugated in thought.

Celia clasped her hands, eyeing the man as though he were a star of the cinema, when in reality he looked to me like the sort of human gumboil she often had lounging at her feet. I mean to say, she'll eventually marry and leave the house, but there's no need for such a kind, gentle girl, a dab hand with a ball of yarn or a paper tied to a bit of twine, to rush too quickly from the parental embrace, is there?

"I do believe I heard something, a door shutting or a heavy tread, as of the footsteps of a substantial sort of person, that penetrated even my sweet dreams." Here Freddie smiled a smile of exceeding fatuousness at Celia, who simpered so hideously in return I promised myself I'd turn a blind eye and cold shoulder on her next overture with paper and string.

At this critical juncture the doorbell rang. Without standing on ceremony—the butler stood with the rest of the domestic staff, huddled in the back hallway like chickens over whom has passed the shadow of a hawk—Lord M threw open the door.

Not unexpectedly, a uniformed officer of the law stood upon the doorstep. "Police Constable Rupert Worple," he announced. "What's all this then? A robbery, you say . . ." His eye fell upon the beauteous Celia. He whisked his hat off his head, revealing a face equipped with granite jaw, clear gaze, and intelligent brow.

Mrs. A stepped into his line of sight like an elephant lumbering into the gunsights. "I've been robbed of a priceless necklace!"

The officer reeled back a pace, then collected himself. "Has anyone left the house since you last saw your necklace?"

"No, not a bit of it," offered Lord Mompesson. "I was just having a word with Thatcher about the wine cellar and saw all the servants, including Mrs. Arbuthnot's maid, gathered in the kitchen."

Ah, the kitchen, I repeated to myself. The domain of Mrs. Beecham. She was, I understand, the despair of the scullery maid, who in the course of her duties had to clear away the bits of meat, fish, and other comestibles that came flying from Mrs. Beecham's expert hands as she worked. But, I ask you, should an artist be expected to keep tidy like lesser mortals? I think not.

"Well then," said P.C. Worple, "if you'd be so good as to collect the servants here in the hall, and show me the scene of the crime."

"Thatcher," Lord Mompesson called to the butler. "See to it."

"Very good, my lord." Thatcher's slicked-back hair and lipless face gave him the appearance of a snake, if not in the

34

grass then amongst the carpets. A fine specimen of a butler he might be, but he regarded the odd hairball, deposited discreetly upon the fringes of the Persian, with a very cold eye, which rather soured my view of him, if you take my meaning.

He began chivvying the staff, including the rotund figure of Mrs. Beecham in her capacious but far from clean apron, and the scrawny one of Mrs. Arbuthnot's maid from their lurking place.

Meanwhile the other humans started up the stairs. I tried to remove my head from between the balusters and found it stuck. "Jasper. . . ."

"Allow me, young Bingo." With the slightest pressure of his teeth, Jasper seized the nape of my neck and pulled me forth like a cork from a bottle. I paused for a moment to smooth my fur back into place. I fancy that its golden color, not to mention the hint of a ruff at my throat, gives me a resemblance to the king of beasts, and no aristocrat should let himself be observed in disarray.

Here came all the pairs of feet clomping up the staircase. Celia paused to tickle my ears—I re-thought my ill-considered impulse to give her the cut direct—and to my surprise, the young Lochinvar of the law offered his sturdy hand to Jasper's discerning nose.

"Come along," said Mrs. Arbuthnot, as Freddie led the way down the corridor in the manner of a hound after a fox—if humans had had tails with which to express themselves, one would have been able to see it upraised in excitement behind him.

Jasper wrinkled his nose. "P.C. Worple smells of soap and toast, a good honest smell. But which of them is scented with that heavy floral odor?"

"That's Mrs. Arbuthnot's perfume," I answered. "Offends the old nostrils like flowers left too long in the vase without a change of water, what? I caught a snootful when she turfed me out of her wardrobe this morning, just as I was settling down for the odd eighty winks on her silk peignoir." "Neither Celia nor Lady Mompesson would deign to pour such an offensive odor upon themselves. Lord Mompesson's bay rum is quite refreshing, considering. . . ." Here Jasper paused, as though putting action to word and considering indeed.

I left him to his cogitations and whiskered down the stairs. The servants were standing about babbling, although not as a brook, merrily. Thatcher stood aloof, displaying his habitual stuffed-frog expression. I slipped between him and the others and aimed for the back hall, thinking that perhaps some morsel of provender had been left unguarded in the kitchen when the Arbuthnot balloon went up. But I was distracted from my purpose by an odd smell.

One of the humans had a bit of an air. It was not Mrs. Beecham, the old dear, who smiled benignly down upon me as I passed. She was scented with her usual glorious fragrance—kipper, beefsteak, and the finest Stilton. Not for nothing does Lord Mompesson resemble a bowl of jelly caught in a stiffish breeze.

Mrs. Arbuthnot's maid, Dolly, stood wringing her hands, her long, thin face set in such deep lineaments of concern that it resembled one or two thoroughbreds of my acquaintance. As her hands met and twisted, they emitted the spicy odor of nutmeg. I'm here to tell you, nutmeg is not one of my favorite flavors—it falls far short of poached salmon or day-old mouse—but I'd not pass up the chance to nip a bit of apple pie from Celia's lovely fingers. Delicately, mind you, never being so inconsiderate as to bite the hand that feeds me.

Nutmeg, it occurred to me as I trotted on down the hall toward the kitchen, was rarely served with breakfast. I cast my tongue's memory back over the array of silver salvers on the sideboard—warm enough to burn the inquisitive nose, I'd discovered once in my impetuous youth. Kedgeree, kidneys, bacon, poached eggs. No nutmeg.

And why should a lady's maid be scented with food at all? This was something to be considered. No need to call on Jasper's deductive abilities. I could solve this mystery myself.

I altered my trajectory and oiled through the half-open door of the pantry. Here amongst the teapots and platters the odor of nutmeg was gaggingly strong. In fact, I discovered by inspecting the sole of my foot, a few grains lay upon the floor. Pulling a face—really, the things one is forced to do upon occasion—I licked the offending bits away and then turned my attention upwards.

It was the work of but a moment to leap upward and land with my usual grace and dignity upon the shelf. The tins and bottles were lined up in good order, like the soldiers standing to attention in one of Lord M's photographs, waiting for the sergeant major to send them into culinary battle. Pepper, mustard, nutmeg. . . .

The solution to the robbery flashed upon me at this point, entire and complete. Dolly had purloined her mistress's jewel and tucked it away, here in the pantry, to be retrieved at her convenience. No wonder the maid's face was etched so deeply with anxiety. It was not anxiety for Mrs. A—indeed, I failed to feel much anxiety for Mrs. A — but for herself.

I nudged the tin of nutmeg to the edge of the shelf and let it fall. Gravity being what it is, the ensuing explosion was most gratifying. The lid of the tin shot out one way, the body another, and the darkish brownish nutmeg spilled across the floor. I sneezed.

When I opened my eyes again, I saw humans standing in the doorway. Celia lifted me from my perch. "Why Bingo, you silly creature. What have you done? I've never known you to put a paw wrong!"

My indignation at being accused of clumsiness was mollified by her embrace. I nestled against her bosom, purringly pleased with my own sagacity. And there are those who say that Bingo has nothing but wax between his ears.

For a long moment P.C. Worple regarded my position, somewhat enviously, I wot. Then, with a shudder as though shaking himself to duty, honor, and country, he squatted down. Withdrawing a pen from his pocket, he lifted something shiny from the fragrant mess. Not the Eye of the Tiger, the big emerald, the object of desire, more's the pity, but a raggedy-looking gold chain.

The Arbuthnot squealed like a train approaching a crossing. "My necklace! The jewel's been ripped from its setting! Infamous, I tell you, infamous!"

"This is Mrs. Beecham's pantry," said Thatcher, his voice dripping doom. "Mr. Quirk averred that he heard the footsteps of a heavy person. Mrs. Beecham must have slipped into Mrs. Arbuthnot's room whilst the household was at breakfast and stolen the jewel. I've always known her to be an untidy and frivolous person, but a thief—I'm shocked, I tell you. Shocked!"

From the hallway, Lord and Lady Mompesson expressed various doubts and disbeliefs. I could almost hear Lord M's avoirdupois deflating. ". . . utter foolishness to imagine a cook of the caliber of Mrs. Beecham would desert her post in the kitchen to go thumping about in people's bedrooms. . . ."

My whiskers went from jaunty to crestfallen, and the purr was stopped in my throat as by a choking hand. The entire sequence of events, set in train by my rashly following up the scent of nutmeg, rose before me like Hamlet's father's ghost.

Once, when Mrs. Beecham went on her well-deserved but much-lamented holiday, Thatcher had employed a relative as a cook. The female Thatcher was lean, pale, sharp, and shared the Thatcher family's disdain for the feline species. She provided Jasper and me with nuggets of noxious brown stuff from a bag labeled, for all I know, "kibbled gravel for terrace restoration."

Never trust someone who's lean, pale, and sharp. Their moral faculties tend to be undernourished. We'd have a pretty thin time of it ourselves if Mrs. Beecham were clapped into chokey, and Thatcher's relative became our cook-in-residence.

"I'll have a word with Mrs. Beecham," said P.C. Worple. Celia, her lovely face furrowed, set me upon the floor, and the humans tottered *en masse* back toward the entrance hall.

I was dashed low at that point, I'm here to say. The sight of Jasper sitting alone in the hall, in the manner of a bit of flotsam left upon the beach by a retreating tide, did little to warm the old cockles. I sneezed again.

"Bless you, young Bingo," said Jasper.

"Bless us both," I retorted, and proceeded to tell him of my ghastly vision of future kibble.

He cocked his head to the side. "I doubt matters will come to that. May I ask what led you here to the pantry, and why you knocked the nutmeg onto the floor? With all due respect to Miss Celia, you hardly did it by accident."

"Well, the dear girl can't always be right, can she? Look

at that loathsome clot Freddie!"

"Of Mr. Quirk, more in a moment, but first. . . ."

"Oh, ah. Yes. I smelled nutmeg on Dolly's hands, and thought that was a dashed rummy sort of thing, a lady's maid quaffing the nutmeg and all."

"Rummy it is, young Bingo." Jasper blinked his amber eyes gravely. "I have encountered a similar conundrum. You may remember how I followed the humans to Mrs. Arbuthnot's bedroom. I was able to slide through the door unobserved by all but Mr. Quirk."

"The loathsome clot," I observed.

"Indubitably. He detected my presence and went so far as to label me 'a filthy beast', at which time he urged me from the room with his foot, much in the manner of a man moving a hassock. I naturally increased my weight proportionally, so that he had to exert more effort than he'd originally intended, and was at last reduced to leaning over and taking hold of my body."

I shuddered at the very image.

"It was however, at that moment I detected upon his hands the same floral odor as that in Mrs. Arbuthnot's wardrobe." Jasper licked his sleek flanks, cleansing them of the befouling touch.

I pride myself upon my quickness of mind. I pounced on his meaning as though upon one of Celia's bits of yarn. "You mean to say he stole her bottle of scent?"

"No," said Jasper, with only the faintest trace of asperity in the angle of his ears, "I mean to say he stole her necklace whilst she was at breakfast with the rest of the humans."

"But, but, I found the necklace here. . . ." I stopped to reconsider. "I found the setting of the necklace is all."

"Indeed, young Bingo. Hidden by the hands of Mrs. Arbuthnot's maid."

Voices came from the entrance hall, Mrs. Beecham's raised in protest, P.C. Worple's calm and cool. It fair gave one the pip to see the old dear distracted from her duties in the kitchen. We definitely needed to find some means of preserving the old status quo.

But I didn't need to inform Jasper of this. "The question," he said, "presents itself in two parts. Firstly, why were the jewel and its setting separated? And secondly, where is the jewel now?"

Jasper in full ratiocinative flow is an inspiring sight. "I hope you intend to point to Thatcher as the culprit."

"As Mr. Thatcher passed by me just now, I took the precaution of sniffing at his hands. They smelled of nothing but freshly-ironed newsprint. I rather suspect that he is merely taking advantage of the situation. No, we have the culprits before our noses—Freddie Quirk and Dolly. Dolly Quirk, I should think. Surely you've taken notice of the resemblance between her and the man I believe to be her brother."

Well, yes, I had noticed they each had a face like a horse, but I hadn't actually taken notice of it, if you catch my meaning. "They're a family of thieves, then, stealing the ocular fixtures of tigers and all."

"So it appears. I daresay Dolly told Freddie that Mrs. Arbuthnot would be visiting Mompesson Hall, whereupon he began chatting up Celia . . ."

"A human chap could hardly avoid chatting up Celia."

". . . so as to be invited for the same weekend. Then he absconded with the jewel, removed it from its setting, and passed the setting on to his sister whilst the other humans were at their morning feed. Unlike either Mrs. Beecham or Mr. Thatcher, the perfidious young woman had a valid reason to be moving about amongst the bedrooms before making her appearance in the kitchen—during the course of which, she hid the aforementioned setting in the pantry."

"To stitch up poor old Mrs. B, do you think?"

"Not necessarily. I expect the Quirks intended to sacrifice the gold setting to draw attention away from themselves and to someone in the household. What they did not intend was for it to come to light quite so quickly. They meant to be far away, with the jewel—or with the proceeds from its sale, rather—when some unwitting bystander or perhaps even an officer of the law opened the tin."

"So Freddie intended to leave Celia high and dry. Tchah!" I said scathingly.

"I daresay Miss Celia would have had the good sense to see past Mr. Quirk's blandishments, not to mention his haberdashery. Really! I ask you!"

Jasper hadn't asked me, but this wasn't the time to debate the whys and wherefores of human clothing. "So what now? Freddie and Dolly can still make their getaway, free and clear as the birds and whatnot."

"Then we must endeavor to stop them. Or him, as I rather suspect it is he who has the jewel." Jasper looked at me.

I looked back. "There's but one thing to do. If it— what's that expression of yours?"

"If it were done when 'tis done, then 'twere well it were done quickly."

"Couldn't put it better myself."

"Then let us position ourselves in the entrance hall."

Passing Thatcher on the way—the man looked like a thundercloud searching for a place to rain—we arrived in the hall just as the other humans were drifting away into various rooms. It appeared as though P.C. Worple, who obviously had a functioning brain cell or two, had taken Mrs.

Beecham into Lord M's study to discuss the matter in a civil fashion, rather than cuffing her ever so capable hands and bunging her straight into chokey.

The Mompessons themselves had gone to ground in the sitting room along with Mrs. Arbuthnot, whose tally-ho had at last dropped to an economical volume. Probably they had requested a restorative, hence Thatcher's mission kitchenwards. The other servants, including, I supposed, the inglorious Dolly, had disappeared. As had the equally inglorious Freddie. . . .

No. Here he came, walking in what he no doubt fancied was a stealthy gait across the upper landing of the staircase, but which to my alert ears sounded like the thud of hoofbeats. He was tucking something away in the inside breast pocket of his jacket.

"Allow me, young Bingo." Jasper shimmered up the stairs.

Freddie started to descend the main flight, his eye darting jerkily to and fro. Halfway down, he encountered Jasper. Or rather, Jasper encountered him, making a quick, expert figure eight through his legs between one step and the next.

Freddie's fall was a thing of beauty and a joy forever, flailing arms and legs and a cry that would strike terror into the heart of a banshee. The cataclysm caused humans to pop out of doorways like an array of cuckoos from their clocks, eyes bulging and mouths open, and gather around the human form now sprawled upon the tiles of the floor.

Jasper shimmered back down the stairs, planted his forefeet upon Freddie's shirt front, dug his claws into the objectionable tie, and then, with a quick fillip of his paw, extracted the something from Freddie's jacket and sent it skittering across the floor.

The object was shiny and green, like a great scarab beetle going on about its business. It was but a small matter for me to show the prowess I'd achieved under Celia's tutelage. I pounced, corralled the stone, and brought it to rest beside P.C. Worple's sensible shoes.

He leaned over and picked it up. "What the . . . Mr. Quirk!"

Freddie groaned. "Filthy beast tripped me up, all of a purpose. . . ."

"Don't be daft," Mrs. Arbuthnot told him. She snatched the stone from Worple's hand and held it aloft, so that it caught the afternoon sunlight and flashed like a veritable— well, it *was* an emerald, dash it all. "The Eye of the Tiger! My family heirloom!"

"Freddie!" said Celia, her lovely complexion flushing a color that would have embarrassed a rose.

"Oh no, Freddie!" yowled a female voice. A rush and stumble amongst the reconvened huddle of servants, and then Thatcher, his meaty hand clasped around her arm, dragged Dolly forward.

"Dolly!" exclaimed Mrs. A "And you came to me with a good reference from Mr. Quirk here. . . . Oh. I see." Her jowls sagged.

Lady Mompesson patted her arm. "There, there, Sadie. All's well that ends well."

Lord M harrumphed. "Blighter, scoundrel, ought to be horsewhipped, uses me, uses my daughter. Uses my cook, for the love of—beyond the pale, I tell you."

"Very true," I said to Jasper.

He stretched and flexed his claws. "If I do say so myself."

P.C. Worple hoicked Freddie to his feet. "Well then. A mighty fine pair of cats you have here, Lord Mompesson.

Lady Mompesson. Miss Celia. . . ." His clear blue gaze stopped at her pink cheeks and hung there.

She smiled at him, a wild surmise lighting her face.

Smoothing her apron, Mrs. Beecham paced past them all and headed down the hall toward the kitchen. "Jewel thieves. Police. It's all upsetting to the digestion. What we all need is a good tea, that'll set us to rights."

Jasper and I cantered on after her, not too quickly, but close enough.

She glanced over her shoulder with a conspiratorial smile. "There you are, you rascals. Funny how you should turn up just when I was thinking of opening a tin of sardines."

Ah yes, I thought, *life is good.*

Beside me Jasper murmured, "Very good, young Bingo. Very good."

Cat Nap

Kristine Kathryn Rusch

She sleeps in the sun, oblivious to all she has wrought. Her white fur glistens in the light, a stark contrast to the rich wood floor beneath her. Occasionally the breeze blowing in through the open window catches her. She raises her small triangular-shaped head, ears up, and sniffs, delicately, as if the air had a bouquet, like wine, that she could accept or reject.

Then she puts her head down, sighs heavily, and falls back to sleep. Her body twitches—dreams, I know—but their content remains a mystery. Does she have nightmares about those days she spent roadside, waiting for someone to find her? Does she run from unseen predators? Cower from yelling voices?

Or are her dreams happy places, filled with hummingbirds and flowers and all the food she can eat?

I do not know and I do not want to know. I like to pretend she is happy here, even in sleep, untormented by memories that would bother humans until the day they died.

The first time I saw her, she was chasing sandpipers on the beach. She was fat and sleek and pampered, so fat that she couldn't catch the birds—probably a good thing, since they would have pecked her to death if she had even come close to them.

For weeks after that, she haunted the beach like a thinning white wraith. I saw her on my daily walks, flitting in and out of the rocks, or sitting roadside and staring at the highway as if waiting for her salvation.

At first I didn't even try to catch her, thinking she belonged to one of the weekenders who filled the beachfront houses every summer. By the time I realized she had been abandoned, I couldn't get to her to come to me. I spent weeks bribing her with food until she learned to trust me.

The day she finally came close enough to let me pet her was the day I scooped her up, put her in the cat carrier I bought just for that purpose, and took her to our small town's only vet. He stitched up gashes on her sides and back, showed me old burns on her paws, and started her on a regimen of pink antibiotics that smelled of bubblegum.

She had no tags, no data chip in her shoulder, nothing to identify her at all. Just a baseball-shaped patch of black on her belly, and eyes so green they looked like they'd been made of emeralds.

No one advertised for her in the papers; no one posted signs for her in the neighborhood. The Humane Society had had no calls from anyone searching for an all-white cat with a patch of black on her belly, and none of the vets for a fifty-mile radius had either.

For good measure, I called the local radio stations, reported her found, and sent notices to newspapers all over the state, promising to return her to anyone who could list her defining characteristics.

No one did. No one even called.

She was mine—and at the time, neither of us was sure we liked the arrangement.

I had come to the Oregon coast with half the fruits of my life's labors, spoils—if you could call them that—of a wretched divorce. It hadn't been acrimonious; it hadn't

47

even been rude; it had just been heartbreakingly empty. Two people arguing over the remains of a life neither of them could live any longer, not with the ghost of their son still haunting the street outside their home.

One particularly bad afternoon, I had gone outside with bleach and a scrub brush, determined to remove the skid marks from the concrete, but as I scrubbed, the liquid turned red.

Suddenly Jesse lay on the road, his small form crumpled and twisted in ways no body should ever be. My wife's screams still echoed in the air, along with the squeal of tires, and that horrible, horrible crash, followed by a thud which, though softer, was somehow worse.

I dropped my scrub brush, and wiped my hands on my jeans, feeling his blood, sticky as it had been that hot summer day, knowing I would never get it off.

That moment—not the accident—was the end. My wife couldn't understand why I wanted to leave the neighborhood. She saw his little frame everywhere, marveled at his happy, smiling face, and heard his laughter. She found comfort in the memories.

I seemed to have lost mine—all but one.

She took the house, and we divided the rest of the assets. I moved to the coast because Jesse could not haunt me there; we weren't going to take him to such a dangerous place until he grew older.

Which wasn't to say I didn't feel him sometimes, just behind me, his soft sweet breath on my shoulder. I would turn, and he would vanish, like a trick of light.

But he was there. I always knew he was there, watching over me, just as I should have watched over him.

The cat and I fell into a routine. Even though I left

kibble in a large bowl, she demanded that I feed her twice a day. I complied. At first, those were the only times she acknowledged me. The rest of the time, she sat in my picture window, staring down at the street.

I wondered what ghosts she saw, what she was hoping for. Often I sat beside her, and stared as well. Sometimes the traffic vanished—the Winnebagos and dusty cars with strange license plates—and all I saw was a single illuminated streetlight, and a small boy, clutching a basketball.

Dad, watch this. Dad—

The cat would flinch, and the image would disappear.

The cat and I would look at each other, as if we were checking to see if the other had had the same vision, and then we would stare once again at the street, watching other people speed to their lives as if they were so much more important than our own.

Gradually, the cat acquired a name.

"How're you, Missy?" I'd say as I carried groceries through the kitchen door.

"Did you sleep well, Missy?" I'd ask when she would show up, threading through my legs, waiting for breakfast.

"What do you see, Missy?" I'd mutter when I sat beside her on our couch, for our evening stare at the street.

She never answered, but it got to the point where she would look at me whenever something that sounded like "missy" came out of my mouth. I had meant the word as a substitute. Somehow it felt rude to call her "cat" when she had a personality all her own.

And she, in turn, gradually warmed to me.

The thaw came in little ways: a chirruped greeting for our evening sessions; a small white face in the kitchen window, waiting for me to come home; the Saturday afternoon she fell asleep, her tiny head resting heavily on my shoe.

But she didn't purr and she didn't cuddle. She rarely came close, and only then to give me instruction—a meow that meant it was nearly time for dinner; a march to the cat box to show me that it was overflowing; a paw on the arm when I stayed up past midnight, to remind me it was time for bed.

It was three months before she slept heavily; six months before she stopped frowning whenever I opened the door, as if she were afraid I would toss her out; nine months before I first heard her purr.

But the purr broke something loose inside her. The next morning, I awoke to find her lying on my chest, her paws kneading my shoulder, my skin wet with drool. She shivered and shuddered and purred so hard I thought she was going to hurt herself. It felt, I later said to a friend, as if she were sobbing a year of pain and anguish away.

I wrapped my arms around her and held her, and she didn't complain or squirm away. In that moment, she became my cat, and I became her person, and neither of us would let anything change that.

The people who abandoned her came back on a Tuesday. I heard rumors that some people were looking for a white cat on Wednesday, but I got confirmation on Thursday, from Missy's vet.

"Thought you'd want to know a couple came in here asking about a white cat with a black stomach," the vet said in a low voice, almost as if the couple were still there. "Said they lost her about a year ago."

"Why are they looking for her now?" I asked.

"They're back in town. They didn't realize she was gone

until they were away from the coast. By then, they weren't sure where they had lost her." The vet's tone made it clear he didn't approve.

"So they just assumed someone took care of her?"

"They're checking," the vet said. "They made it sound like they've been looking all year."

"But you don't believe them?"

"Maybe one of them has," the vet said. "But Missy had a lot of old scars. She didn't get those from being lost."

"She was also fat and sleek when I first saw her. Someone obviously fed her and groomed her."

"Who knows? Maybe she was a stray before they got her," the vet said. "All I'm doing is letting you know they're here. I didn't mention you. I have their number if you want to contact them. But I'd think about it, I really would. Sometimes one half of a couple really loves an animal, and the other half uses that animal as leverage. I think Missy's a lot better off with you."

I liked to think that too. But Missy did cast longing gazes at the street, even now. I thought she was still pining for someone, someone whom she really and truly loved.

Yet, for one year, these people never called. They never checked with the Humane Society. They never did anything that made me believe she was precious to them.

I never asked the couple's name, and I ignored the paper flyers that appeared all over town with a picture of cat—perhaps Missy—on them.

She was an indoor cat who had her own life now. She was mine. And she still spent her mornings shuddering and sighing on my chest, as if I were the only safe place in her entire world.

Oregon coastal towns seem big to tourists because most

tourists come here when the towns are stuffed. The hotels are full; the streets are full; the restaurants are full. But in truth, coastal towns are tiny things—the largest only having a handful of locals year-round.

The locals all know each other, and usually that's a good thing.

Sometimes it isn't.

Someone clearly told Missy's former owners about me. I have no idea who, even to this day, and I'm never going to try to find out. But less than a week after they blew back into town, Missy's former owners showed up on my doorstep.

Fortunately I was home. If I hadn't been, they might have taken Missy, and I would never have known what happened to her. Unlike them, though, I would have searched immediately, done all I could to find her, done everything in my power to make certain she was all right.

I knew who was at my door the moment the bell rang. Call it prescience if you will, or perhaps simple deductive reasoning. None of my local friends used the bell. The delivery services left packages outside the door, and no one else came to my house.

Missy ran from the unfamiliar noise. I waited until she was gone before I pulled the door open.

I have no idea what I expected. I had built these people up in my mind into something horrible—people who abused animals; people who didn't care—but they seemed normal. He was tall and thin, awkward in an out-of-date suit, and she was short and round, with grandmotherly curls and a delicately lined face.

They were in their seventies at the very youngest, and that surprised me.

"Mr. Triwell?" the man asked. Polite, but then, you'd

expect polite from someone of his generation.

"Yes?" I said, pretending I didn't know what this was about.

"I understand you have our cat."

The sympathy their appearance engendered, the momentary lapse in which I actually thought I could talk with these people, vanished.

"Your cat?" I said, pretending ignorance again.

"Yes." The woman stepped forward and peered around me, as if she were looking for Missy. Missy had been her cat, not his. I could tell from the longing in her face, the softness around her eyes. "We heard you found her. I— we—"

"We can pay you for your trouble," the man said.

"I'm sorry," I said, biting back anger. Where did they get the right to barge into our lives and pretend like nothing happened. "I have no idea what you're talking about."

"Arabella," the woman said, her voice a coo. She was answering my query and calling the cat at the same time. "We lost her last year, and even though I looked for her, I—we— couldn't find her. We've been searching everywhere."

"Really?" I crossed my arms, hoping Missy wouldn't appear. I blocked the woman's view of the door. "Last year? Did you call the vets? The Humane Society? Did you do anything at all to help this cat survive a year outside?"

"So you do have her," the man said with deliberate obtuseness. "We'll take her now."

"I never said I had your cat," I snapped, and slammed the door shut. Then I turned and leaned against it. Missy hadn't appeared after all, but I felt an irrational fear, the kind that used to plague me after Jesse died. Maybe Missy had slipped out while I was talking to those people. Maybe she was going to get lost all over again.

Even though I knew that was nonsense. Even if Missy had slipped out, someone would find her. She wore a collar now, even though she was an indoor cat, and I had gotten her an I.D. chip. Missy would never get lost again.

Still, I searched for her and found her in her favorite hiding place—beneath my bed. She stared at me with wide eyes, and I could sense fear.

I just didn't know if it was hers or mine.

They came back several more times, and I never again opened the door to them. I stayed home so that they wouldn't be able to sneak inside and steal her. For some reason, I put nothing past these people.

I ran an antiquarian bookshop by appointment only, and during that week, I left it closed, canceling what few appointments I had. Missy had become the most important thing in my life, and I wasn't going to let these people, no matter who they were, take her away from me.

Even though I didn't leave the house, I learned several things. I found out that the couple lived in a giant recreational vehicle—the kind that is a moving home on wheels. Their names were Kilpatrick, and they had been coming to the coast for two weeks every summer for fifteen years.

Locals did remember them. They also remembered a dog the couple had had—a small, yapping dog, the subject of many complaints. The dog did not return the following summer. From that point on, the Kilpatricks had cats—never one the same.

The woman doted on them. The man couldn't care less. Apparently, they had had Missy for two summers, since one or two of the other summer residents of the RV park remembered her peering out of the window of the RV's main bedroom long before she became a resident of the streets.

Missy was peering out one of my bedroom windows when the Kilpatricks returned for the last time. She squealed and jumped to the floor, running for my bed. I saw her go by my study, her ears flattened, her body low to the ground. I knew someone was outside even before the doorbell rang.

I debated answering. The bell rang again, and I finally went to the door. As I entered the living room, an envelope fell through the old mail slot and slid across the hardwood floor.

I pulled the door open to see Mr. Kilpatrick get into an ancient Cadillac. He put the car into gear and pulled into the street without checking his mirrors, peeling off before I could stop him.

My breath caught and my heart pounded. The man was a reckless driver on top of everything else. After Jesse had died because a driver had gone too fast down our suburban street, too fast to stop, too fast to even honk before Jesse rolled over the hood, smashed his window, and rolled off the back of the car, I had no tolerance for any kind of recklessness behind the wheel.

I eased my door closed and walked to the couch where Missy and I spent our evenings. I sat down gingerly, turning the envelope over and over in my hands.

My name was written across it in precise, spidery writing. I slipped my finger under the flap, and found that it hadn't been well sealed. The envelope opened easily.

The letter inside was written on expensive but yellowing paper, with a law firm's logo embossed into the fibers themselves. The law firm's name, *Kilpatrick and Associates*, was printed along the top, followed by an address in Denver, Colorado. The address was so old that it had no zip code, and the phone number below used letters instead of numbers as its first three characters.

The street address had been crossed out, leaving only the Post Office box, and a zip code had been written in.

The letter itself was typed on a manual typewriter.

Mr. Triwell:

We have attempted to contact you many times. You refuse to see us about our cat, Arabella, whom you have cared for this past year.

While we appreciate the care you have given Arabella, she is ours, and we would like her returned. We will take this to court if we have to. You may not be aware that there is precedent in Oregon which favors the original owner of any pet in a custody dispute.

Please return Arabella to us so that we may settle this amiably.

John D. Kilpatrick
Attorney at Law

My stomach twisted, and I clutched the letter closely. I was familiar with the case he referred to. People still talked about it whenever someone took in a stray animal.

Several years ago, a man found a Jack Russell terrier on a beach in Seaside. He took the terrier to the animal shelter. When no one claimed the dog, he legally adopted it. Months later, the original owner contacted him, claiming she had been out of town and a caretaker had lost the dog. The new owner refused to give the dog back. The case went to court, and the terrier went home with his original owner.

Since then, two other cases had been tried over similar circumstances—one here in Seavy County—and had been settled for the original owners each time.

It was clear that Missy had been theirs initially. I had no

idea why they were fighting so hard for her return now when they hadn't seemed to care for her before.

I folded the letter in my pocket, and called my neighbor to ask her to watch the house for any suspicious activity, requesting that she call me on my cell phone should anything happen. Then I left, locking up tight, and I walked to the RV park near the beach access at the bottom of the hill.

It wasn't hard to find the Kilpatrick's superdeluxe RV because it had been described to me so many times. It was parked near the mouth of the park, and was not plugged into the water or electric services. The RV looked like it was ready to leave, not like it was here for the long haul.

Outside, a grill was cooling, the charcoal inside turning to ash. The metal rack on top was still covered with fat from the meat cooked for that day's lunch. A half empty beer bottle of Heineken leaned against one of the legs, long forgotten.

I mounted the metal steps beneath the pull-out awning, and knocked.

After a moment, the door opened. Mr. Kilpatrick blocked my entrance.

"So," he said, "changed your mind?"

"I'd like to talk with you," I said.

He stepped aside to let me in, but he left the door open, as if he didn't trust me. Old scents of garlic, onions, and cooked meat filled the small living area. Mrs. Kilpatrick stood in the nearby kitchen, dry-wiping dishes. She set down a large cast iron skillet when she saw me.

"You have Arabella?" Her voice was soft and I heard hope in her voice.

"I don't have a cat with me," I said, still unwilling to admit that Missy was theirs. "What I do want to know is why it took you a year to start searching for yours."

Mrs. Kilpatrick looked at her husband.

"That's not your concern," he said.

"It is if you threaten to sue me for custody of my cat," I said.

"Our cat," he said.

"We tried to look for her." Mrs. Kilpatrick's voice rose over his. He shot her an angry glare. "We just—couldn't find her."

"A year," I said. "No contact to the shelters. No contact with the vets. All the stuff you're doing now you could have done then."

"We did," she said.

"I checked," I said. "No one ever asked about a white cat with a black belly."

Mrs. Kilpatrick looked at her husband, and her face went pale. "You said you called. You said—"

"Shut up," he said. "What matters is she's our cat, and we'll do what we can to get her."

"Why?" I asked. "It's clear you don't care for her. It's clear you never have. How did she get those burn marks on her paws, anyway?"

The question came out before I could stop it, and I cursed silently. It was a tacit admission that I had the cat they wanted.

"Burn marks?" Mrs. Kilpatrick's voice rose again. "She had burn marks?"

"Old scars on her paws," I said. The mistake was made. There wasn't much I could do to correct it. "They had nothing to do with her weeks of starvation. They happened when she lived with her previous owner."

Tears filled her eyes, and before I realized what she was doing, she grabbed the cast iron skillet with both hands and swung it like a club. It hit Mr. Kilpatrick so hard that it made a smacking sound, like grapefruit dropped on concrete. He stood for half a second, his eyes suddenly empty, and then fell forward.

I had to step aside to keep him from landing in my arms. His head thumped against weather stripping, his mouth open and dripping blood. The back of his skull was a mass of bone, black blood, and thinning hair.

His eyes were open. He was dead. I knew it as clearly as I had known Jesse was dead. Sometimes checking for breath, for a pulse, was simply redundant.

"You're a rich man, aren't you, Mr. Triwell?" Mrs. Kilpatrick asked. Her voice sounded reasonable again. In fact, if I weren't looking at her, I would have thought she was an extremely rational woman.

But she was standing next to her husband's body, holding a skillet like a baseball bat, as if she were waiting for someone to throw another pitch. Her face was covered with a fine spray of blood, and her hair had come free of the tight bun that had held it in place.

I had no idea what she planned next. That, and sheer shock made me answer her.

"No," I said.

"The house, your bookstore. You have money." Her voice wasn't reasonable. It was flat. I had mistaken softness for calm.

"I suppose it might look that way." I waved a hand toward her husband. "We have to help him. Where's your phone?"

"We don't have one," she said. "We can't afford it. Just like we can't afford a parking space here. They're going to make us move. John can't manipulate them any more. He used to be so good at manipulating, after the law firm went under. But people don't see him any more, so they won't listen to the promises. They just see an old man now, and they all think old men are poor. And we are."

She blinked, then looked at me. The tears still floated in her eyes.

"He just wanted your money." She sounded so disappointed. "I thought this time he was actually doing it for me. For Arabella. But I should have known after he kicked Daisy like that. I should have known he couldn't care about anyone but himself."

"Daisy was your dog?" I had to keep her talking while I backed out the door. She wasn't thinking clearly, and I needed to get out of there, needed to get help.

"My dog. The animals were mine. They always ran away. He said they hated me." A tear ran down her cheek. "All but Daisy. She wouldn't leave, so he kicked her. And kicked her. And kicked her. Arabella hid from him. But not enough."

My left foot found the second step, and I put my weight on it. Then I jumped to the ground, away from that skillet.

"I'm getting help," I said, and ran.

I ran to the office, called the authorities and waited. They showed up a few minutes later. An officer stayed with me while others went to find Mrs. Kilpatrick. They arrested her and took his body away.

Then they asked me why I had been in the RV, and I told them about everything but the letter, which remained in my pocket until I got home. Then I tore up the letter and flushed it down the toilet.

Even without the letter, it wasn't hard to verify my story. Every local in town knew about Missy and the Kilpatricks' strange arrival one year later.

The police stated, and some psychiatrist agreed, that my arrival at the RV was a catalyst for years of repressed anger on Mrs. Kilpatrick's part. She had clearly loved her animals—they had been a substitution for her children—and her husband's abuse and murder of them had been more than she could bear.

When she learned that he had done the same thing to a cat she had loved beyond all others, as well as lied to her about trying to find it, then doing a reversal by setting up a blackmail scheme with me, she had snapped.

The blackmail was just a guess, of course. The lawsuit—which I never mentioned—probably would not have happened. Kilpatrick would probably have settled with me for an undisclosed sum. I had ruined his plan by coming to the RV and confronting him in front of his wife.

As a catalyst, I did feel responsible. I found Mrs. Kilpatrick a good lawyer who was willing to work *pro bono*. Under his advice, she claimed she suffered from battered spouse syndrome, and pleaded to a lesser charge. She was given probation and placed in a resident care facility, the profits from the sale of her RV and her belongings providing her entry fee.

I intervened one more time, making sure that the home had a program that involved pets. People brought specially trained dogs and cats once a week, and apparently that was the highlight of Mrs. Kilpatrick's new life.

She asked me for Missy—Arabella as she called her—but I couldn't part with my girl. I knew there had been a bond between them; that had been clear in Missy's longing for her owner. But I also knew that victims of batterers often learn to batter.

I couldn't risk Missy's life with a woman who had murdered her own husband.

★ ★ ★ ★ ★

I wonder what she would think of all this, my pretty little white cat with the black spot on her belly. As we sit at night on our couch and stare into the street, I think of ways to talk with her.

But Missy, for all her intelligence, is not a child. She cannot tell me what she wants. She can only tell me how she feels.

She still runs when the door opens, and she's terrified of the outdoors. She avoids hot objects, and she purrs at the sound of female voices.

But she cuddles with me now, and in the mornings, she crawls into my arms, seeking comfort. I think she has nightmares of being alone, of being abandoned, of being tortured by the husband of the woman who loved her.

I have never allowed anyone to speak of the tragedy in Missy's presence, nor have I brought copies of the local paper into the house. I kept the radio off until the case ended.

I know that cats aren't human. I know that they have different brains, different ways of perceiving the world. But I also know that Missy understands language—certain words and sounds, such as her name, mean something to her. I believe she heard Mrs. Kilpatrick call for her that day, and I believe that Missy remained under the bed.

Not even love could triumph over the hurts my poor cat suffered.

And I do not want her to suffer any more. So we spend as much time together as I can manage, living our quiet little lives. She remains in her house, and I stay in my small town, letting our boundaries define our existence.

I watch her sleep and pray she is dreaming of happy things, of hummingbirds and flowers and all the food she can eat. I like to pretend she is happy here, even in sleep, untormented by memories that will bother me until the day I die.

The Breath of Bast

P. N. Elrod

Charles Escott smiled across his uncluttered desk at a potential client. "May I inquire as to who referred you to me, Miss Selk?"

Cassandra Selk was what his part-time partner in the Escott Agency would have called "a knockout in heels." Possessed of raven-black hair and expressive eyes so brown as to be black as well, Escott's first thought when he ushered her into his office was that she was an artist's model. As it turned out, she was herself an artist, a famous one. He was chagrined that he'd never heard of her, but she didn't seem to mind; apparently few outside of certain rarified circles were familiar with her name. Her area of expertise was sculpture; her favorite subject was cats, and she sold them all over the world.

Miss Selk's remarkable eyes seemed to shimmer. "Mrs. Wasserman spoke highly of your efficiency and attention to detail. *And* your sympathy toward animals."

Mrs. Wasserman's business was still fresh in Escott's mind. He'd agreed to kidnap her dog from her estranged husband. Hardly a case to test one's intellectual talents, but that sort of mundane job paid the bills. Besides, Escott liked dogs. "Yes, the little canine was a most agreeable travel-companion. Have you a similar task in mind?"

Miss Selk shook her head. "I require a dropping-off, not a picking-up."

"May I have more details?" He hoped she would take her

time; he wanted to extend his enjoyment of her altogether fascinating face.

"Hm?" She blinked. "Yes, of course. I've completed a commission for a local collector. I need you to deliver it, then return to tell me her reaction to my work."

His smile faltered. "Why not employ a regular delivery service?"

"I want someone with an eye for detail and a good memory to make a full and complete report."

"Of the collector's reaction? I see." He didn't, but would never admit it aloud. "Why not go yourself?"

Her bewitching smile melted into one of rueful sadness. "It's impossible because of my severe allergy to cats. This collector has at least a dozen running about her house, and I dare not set foot to the threshold. It's terrible for me because I absolutely adore them. They're such beautiful, graceful, *noble* creatures, don't you think?"

"Oh, yes, I've always thought so. You say they are your specialty? What do you do for models?"

"I rely on photographs; many artists do so. The difference for me is making a three-dimensional creation from a two-dimensional image. The dynamics are fascinating."

"Is it not frustrating being unable to work from a live model?"

Her eyes shimmered again, as though she'd heard that question many times. "Not really. From conversations I've had with photographers, it's very difficult to get a cat to hold still for anything. On the other hand, I've been compared to Beethoven. I'm unable to be in the same room with my favorite animal just as he was unable to hear his own music."

"That is ironic."

"I've had years to consider the irony and concluded that

if I did not have this allergy, then I would have a house full of cats and not one piece of sculpture. Without what some would call a defect, I should be leading quite a bit different life, perhaps not as fulfilling."

Escott found himself warming nicely to her turn of mind, which he found as interesting as her looks. However, this was a business transaction, so he gently asked a few more questions and said he would be pleased to take on the errand. Miss Selk—she asked him to *please* call her Cassandra—signed his standard contract and they shook hands.

"The sculpture is in my car," she said. "It's not large, if you . . ."

He assured her he would be delighted to fetch it.

On this humble Chicago street close to the Stockyards there was no question about which car was hers. The 1937 Cadillacs were still barely off the assembly line, but she had one. That, combined with Cassandra's expensive fur coat and silk dress, belied any doubts Escott harbored about whether she could afford his standard fee. He retrieved a small, heavy wooden box and carried it up to his second floor office, placing it carefully on his desk.

"Would you like to see it?" she asked, eyes bright with pride.

"Very much." After she left he'd planned to open it to answer his own curiosity and as a precaution. In his line of business, which required that he undertake odd and frequently unpleasant errands between parties in disagreement, it was only prudent. So far he'd not been employed to deliver a bomb for some crazed anarchist, but there was a first time for everything.

The box was just over a foot tall, the top not nailed in place, but fitting like a lid. Cassandra lifted it off, revealing a tangled nest of excelsior.

"I'm afraid it will make a mess," she said.

"Easily cleaned." He pulled out handfuls of the stuff until encountering something very hard. Cold metal, with dulled points, he thought.

"Just take it out by the head. It won't break."

He did so, brushing away more excelsior. "My heavens."

He reverently set the object on his desk. He was no expert in the field, but possessed an instinct for genius, and that was what shone before him. The metal statue was that of a proudly seated feline done in the Egyptian style. For all he could tell, it might have come right from some ancient temple. Hieroglyphs were incised into the cat's body and along the base upon which it rested.

"Is it silver?" he asked, eyeing its regal head. The points he'd felt had been the ears.

"Yes." She seemed pleased with his obvious awe of her work. "I normally cast in other metals when I use them as my medium, but this was a special commission, and I'm sure you're aware that the client is always right."

"Indeed." On visits to Chicago's museums Escott often found himself mesmerized by certain pieces. He was aware of his own artistic streak, expressed, once upon a time, by being on the stage in his youth. In those early years of knocking around with a traveling repertory company he learned how to create a realistic illusion out of next to nothing. Those illusions lasted only for the duration of the performance, though. Such work gave him a sharp appreciation for individuals whose talent could make a lasting creation. "This is exquisite. Perhaps sometime you could let me see more of—"

"Yes, of course. Tonight, if you'd like—after you make the delivery."

He looked at her, slightly startled at this display of repressed eagerness. Certainly he found her attractive, but was this a reciprocation of a like feeling on her part or merely a desire to show off to an appreciative audience? He was not inexperienced when it came to artists and their egos. The fact that she wanted a full description of her client's reaction indicated that Cassandra possessed a sizable vanity concerning her work. But then this cat sculpture was evidence enough that its creator had earned the right to indulge. Well, he would find out later tonight.

The delivery went smoothly. A somber butler took Escott into the depths of an enormous house where he met the client and several of her cats in a lush drawing room. With a proper flourish—for he understood the importance of a proper presentation—Escott placed the Egyptian-style work on a central table and duly observed every nuance of reaction. The woman waxed long in her praise for Cassandra Selk.

"It's perfect, *exactly* what I wanted," she said. "I've commissioned similar works from others, but only Cassandra truly understands. The hieroglyphs are all real, you know. I wrote them out for her to copy, and she got them right! Every last one of them. I think I shall get rid of the others, now. I shan't allow lesser works to share the same room with this piece."

"Indeed," he said. Three of her cats busily wound themselves in a friendly way around Escott's legs, their tails straight up with a small crook at the end.

"Goodness, they do seem to like you."

He smiled good-naturedly down at his furry worshippers. "I like them."

The client turned back to her acquisition, a dreamy look on her soft features. "Cassandra has a remarkable perception about this period, though that's hardly a surprise, as you know."

Escott realized she did not understand he was a hired agent, and had taken him for one of Cassandra's friends. Curiosity led him to encourage the misapprehension. "I'm amazed by it," he said agreeably.

"Her past life during that time must have been marvelous. She retains so much memory of it. Such a strong soul."

"Indeed?" *This* was an odd turn.

"But then one would have to be for the gods to choose her for one of their high priestesses. It's a great responsibility. What a pity she wavered in her vows by falling in love with a priest of Ra and he with her. Such a punishment to live this life allergic to these dear ones." She stroked the silver cat as though it were one of the live specimens loafing and prowling about the room.

Escott read a lot, including a certain amount on esoteric topics, so he wasn't totally at sea, but he did not know what sort of response was expected to this revelation. He settled for making a sympathetic noise.

"Yes," she continued with a sigh. "We ordinary mortals are allowed our little mistakes and can obtain forgiveness, but those chosen by the gods are not let off so easily. I think Cassandra has dealt marvelously with her punishment, though. Surely by such an outpouring of work in this life she will have proved to them her sincere atonement, don't you think?"

"Oh, absolutely," he said, with much confidence. He wondered if this was the client's own fancy or if Cassandra also shared it. He suspected this lady had seen that film—what was it?—*The Mummy,* one too many times.

A cat of the Abyssinian breed leapt lightly up on the

table, nosed the sculpture, then jumped on Escott, who was just quick enough to catch the lithe animal in his arms.

His hostess gaped. "I'm sorry. That's Ma'at. She's usually very reserved with guests."

He managed to keep Ma'at from mauling his suit in her endeavor to burrow inside his coat. She purred like an idling car. "How flattering. I hope she doesn't expect to go home with me."

"Oh, you won't budge her from the house, but I've never seen her take to anyone so quickly before. It's quite astonishing."

Escott noted that Ma'at's claws were dug deep into his nearly new single-breasted coat. He refrained from pulling her off since forcing a cat to do something was always unwise; she would let go when she was ready. It seemed prudent to continue holding her for the rest of his brief visit. And anyway, the purring was pleasant.

Miss Cassandra Selk lived in another large house halfway across Chicago. Escott knew he had the right place; a dozen terracotta lions guarded the walkway path, each in a different pose, and two uncannily realistic life-sized ceramic leopards crouched on either side of the entry.

Cassandra had changed from her furs and silk dress into a white silk lounging outfit. It was diaphanous, but cunningly pleated so the many layers concealed everything, yet at the same time revealed much. Rather too much for a formal interview, he thought. As the sole owner of his agency Escott could dictate whether or not fraternization with clients was appropriate on any given case. This commission was all but completed, though. Escott thought he knew what she was doing, and composed himself to agree with everything. After all, the client was always right.

Her home reflected her inner creative drive; cats were everywhere. When he asked, she replied with pride that yes, she had sculpted all of them.

"There are so many different artistic styles," he said. "My understanding is that an artist strives to perfect his or her own expression."

"I do that, but I also enjoy exploring the various modes of the past. Each age looked on cats in their own way, and it helps me to understand those lost worlds better when I create something that could have come from a long dead time. Of course, my modern efforts are signed and dated, so I'm in no danger of being accused of forgery."

"You display an amazing range." Escott compared an elongated Celtic-style carving to one with a distinct Chinese ancestry. "I could swear that these were done by two different artists."

"It took years of study and experimentation." She invited him to sit on her couch, and he accepted her offer of sherry. "What I have here are my best efforts, the ones I can't bear to sell. As you can see, the Egyptian style is my favorite. It's so clean and pure in form, yet can be both staid and playful, depending on one's approach . . ." Her enthusiasm for her craft made her pale face light up, creating a hypnotic contrast to her dark hair and eyes.

Eventually they took a tour of her home. It was better than a museum, for she was able to tell exactly how she'd made each of her works, pointing out details he might otherwise have missed. By the time they'd returned to her parlor she sat next to him in a most cozy and unaffected manner.

Cassandra plied him with more sherry and finally asked about her client's reaction to the statue. Escott gave her a full report.

He concluded: "She told me that you must phone tomorrow so she may express her pleasure personally."

"Of course. I'm relieved I got the hieroglyphics right. Sometimes taking a commission is a thankless task. A client's vision is often totally different from what's in my mind. They are rarely able to describe *what* they want, and more than once I've had pieces rejected because of the client's own confusion—for which I would get the blame. When an acceptance like this happens it's something to celebrate."

Escott congratulated her and privately wondered if she would mind very much if he kissed her. They were quite close together on her couch. *Not quite yet*, his inner instinct told him. He expected she would let him know when she was ready.

"Would you like to see my studio?" she asked.

"Very much."

Standing up was almost embarrassing, but he managed not to sway from a wave of dizziness. Normally two small sherries wouldn't faze him, but he'd forgotten to eat again. Perhaps that was a good thing. He could ask Cassandra to a late dinner. It shouldn't take her long to change from her outfit. It looked as though an easy tug on one of the ties would have the whole thing off in a trice.

Happy thought, that.

Cassandra led him down to what would be a basement in any other house. This one had been reconstructed to her needs, though. The ceiling was twelve feet high and decoratively painted. This time the Egyptian influence was undiluted. Birds, flowers, rushes, palm trees, and papyrus plants brought the smooth plaster walls to startling life.

"This is no studio," he said, entranced. "It is art itself."

"I knew you would feel it, too," she said. "Let me show you where I work."

But as she led him in he saw no sculpting tools, no kiln, no boxes of supplies, no piles of raw clay kept damp under protective cloth, no works in progress, not even a sketch book. This broad room was more like an extravagant film set. Rows of torches marched along its walls. Though their light was obviously electrical, the anachronistic bulbs were carefully concealed by yellow and red tinted glass shaped to look like flames. Some mechanism for the current made them flicker, giving the effect of fire.

At the far end of the chamber stood two tall guardian cats of painted terracotta, larger yet still-elegant versions of the silver one he'd delivered. Between them, standing on its end was a—oh, God, that couldn't be right—a mummy case? It was open, and within lay a man-shaped form wrapped with dusty gray bandages.

"You look a little overwhelmed," said Cassandra. "Here . . . sit down a moment." She eased him onto a low, wide bench covered with hieroglyphics, many of them picked out in gold leaf.

"I-I might mar the finish."

"It's all right," she assured him. "There, that's much better."

He had to admit that his dizziness was turning into a great nuisance. Unless he could get it under control this evening would have an ignominious finish. What would she think of him, getting drunk on just two—

No, impossible. Even on an empty stomach.

His inner alarm bells rang loud and long, yet he felt strangely distanced from them, strangely slowed. There was a terrific emergency he had to see to, but it seemed miles away. Someone else would deal with it, he was sure.

Smiling down at him beatifically, Cassandra persuaded him to stretch full length upon that low bench. She really

73

was quite breathtaking in the flickering light. For a moment he thought she would kiss him, but she moved out of his rapidly blurring view.

He called after her, futilely. She didn't come back.

God, he was so tired.

The drink, Hamlet, the drink. . . .

Queen Gertrude's words as she succumbed to poison drifted through his mind. That had always been a hard scene to pull off well. The audience was focused on the excitement of the duel, and then Gertrude had to shift their attention and sympathy over to her. Not easy, but with the right actress . . .

Escott shook his head violently. It made him more dizzy, but woke him up a bit. Right. He had to get out of here. Find some fresh air. He'd send Miss Selk a bill, and that would be the end of it.

But when he tried to sit up, he found his arms to be snugly bound to . . . to . . . he wasn't sure what, but it wasn't allowing him much movement.

Oh, dear. This was bad.

His surge of panic helped clear his muzzy head enough to stay awake. He had a presentiment that sleeping in this place would prove fatal. Where was Cassandra?

Escott shoved his immediate terror down deep and concentrated on getting loose from the bench or altar or whatever it was. He didn't want to think of it as an altar, for that implied a sacrifice of some sort.

Bloody hell . . .

He struggled to slip free, and when that didn't work, he tried to make slack instead. That tightened his bonds, but allowed him movement. By some hard and painful twisting, he was able to get a hand inside his waistcoat pocket where he always kept a penknife. No longer used to cut quill pens, it served to open his mail, and hopefully the blade would be sharp enough to sever these . . . bandages?

His guts swooped at the sight of so many layers of narrow, wheat-colored linen wrapping his wrists. He looked like a recovering suicide. Careful not to drop the knife, he got the blade open using his thumbnail and began awkwardly sawing away. He couldn't see what he was cutting or feel much. His hand was numb. Had to work fast, before he lost all feeling, before Cassandra—

He froze at the soft sound of a door opening. Should he pretend to be unconscious? No, better to try talking to her.

She glided close, bare feet whispering against the floor. They darted in and out from the long hem of her gown like shy doves. She wore the same pleated silk garment, but had added wrist cuffs covered with glittering stones, a jeweled belt, and a wide pectoral collar on her shoulders. She'd arranged her black hair so that it hung straight, held back from her face by a gold forehead band. He wasn't sure how historically accurate it might be, but she did look impressive.

Please, God, don't let her notice the knife. He thought his fingers were closed over it, but couldn't tell.

"Hello," he said, as though nothing was amiss. He was surprised at how calm he sounded. All that stage training . . .

"Hello," she responded, her tone warm and loving. "Don't be afraid."

"Oh, not at all." Improvisation had never been his strong suit on stage, but it seemed to work well enough here. Desperation turning to inspiration, that had to be it. "Is everything going well?"

She caught her breath, fingers to her red-painted mouth. "I knew, I just *knew* you were the one."

"Of course I must be. Your insight is uncanny."

"But I've been misled before. Those who have tried to keep us apart interfered, but I have at last been guided to the clear path. Oh, my love, it's been such a long and terrible wait."

"It has. But it's over now. Please, raise me up that I might embrace you." He hoped this was what she wanted to hear.

Her eyes fairly blazed with exultation. "Yes, oh, yes! Soon, my love. Soon we will join. Bast has forgiven our transgression. She knows that the world is changed and her chosen ones must change with it. In this life we *can* be together. That which was once forbidden now has her blessing."

"How glad I am. My heart sings from it, but I'm not sure I remember everything. . . ." He'd begun sawing at the linen bindings again. If he could keep her talking long enough, distracted long enough. . . .

Cassandra seemed as fixed on her delusion as she was about her art. "My poor love, of course you can't remember, not until you are made whole again. In his rage Ra struck with his sword of gold and sundered your *ka* in twain. Only part of you lives on in this body; your other half was preserved until such time as Bast could persuade Ra to forgive you as she forgave me."

Just who or what does she think is in that mummy case? "I deserved mighty Ra's wrath, did I not?"

"It has followed you through many lifetimes. Bast revealed them to me, but your suffering is about to end."

He didn't care for the sound of that. "What glad news. How will you—ah—heal me?"

"You shall see, my dearest of all dear hearts. You'll have but the briefest moment of darkness. In that moment your *ka* will return to you, and you'll wake again whole and well."

"I'm looking forward to it. Each word you speak seems to open my memory. But these bindings are too tight and quite unnecessary. Please, take them away that I may give my *ka* a proper welcome."

She stroked his brow with cool fingers. "Soon. Your hold on this life may overpower your willingness to surrender to the next. There are vast forces at work against us. *This* time we will prevail. This time I *will* get the ceremony right. There is nothing to fear."

He held to a brave loving face until she walked from view, then fought another swift jolt of panic. He doubled his sawing efforts, but couldn't feel anything of his fingers; for all he could tell he could be cutting the wrong bit of fabric.

Cassandra was somewhere by the mummy case, half-chanting, half-singing words he couldn't understand. Occasionally the name *Bast* cropped up, and twice he heard *Ra* mentioned. Their latter-day priestess began pacing around the chamber, carrying a shallow bowl filled with aromatic incense. Clouds of the stuff filled every corner. He hoped it would obscure her vision, for now he was being anything but subtle in trying to cut the bandaging.

Then Cassandra appeared next to him. Her eyes watered freely from the smoke, but she seemed elated. "They have heard my prayers."

"Good," he said, resisting the urge to cough. "I feel my *ka* approaching across the darkness."

"Not yet. Just one more moment. . . ."

She bent and pulled up a thick and heavy cushion. It was embroidered with more Egyptian motifs. She raised it high like an offering, and called for Bast and Ra to bless what she was about to do.

Abrupt comprehension as to what that would be flooded him. He threw all his strength into tearing his arm free, but though there was some give, the bindings remained fast.

"Cassandra!"

She looked down.

He spoke quickly, trying to keep up with a burst of an idea engendered by her watering eyes. "I beg of you a boon. Something to give me courage in the darkness, for my fear is great." No lie in that.

"What? The gods won't be put off."

"They will for this, they understand. Please, love, let me kiss you on *this* side of the veil."

She hesitated. "But why? Soon we will—"

"It's for you! Once I have passed through the darkness, once my *ka* has returned, I will kiss you again, and then you will be certain my sundering has been healed. You will *know!*"

Cassandra lowered the cushion. "Oh, if I had doubts before they flee from me now. You *are* the one!"

With that, she fairly flung herself upon him. In turn, he managed to summon up an illusion of feeling for her. He hoped she would mistake it for sincere passion rather than shuddering terror. It helped that she helped. Her anticipation for his soul's restoration had apparently gotten her well into a state of arousal.

He put everything he had into their kiss, and prayed it would be enough. Eventually she collapsed breathless onto his chest, holding him tight. Better and better.

"Soon," she muttered into his coat, which still bore a liberal coating of Ma'at's fur. "Very, very soon."

After a moment, she dragged away, wiping her wet cheeks. Her eyes streamed tears, yet she smiled through them. She sneezed, messily, and grabbed his breast pocket handkerchief. Repairs took a little time and didn't seem to help. Her kohl-outlined eyes were red and puffy.

"How sweet it will be for us both." Her voice had grown thick with emotion, but her arms were steady as she picked the cushion up. She raised it again, then brought it down hard on Escott's face.

He struggled, wrenching to one side, trying to draw air, but his mouth and nose were wholly covered. There was no escape. If he could just hold his breath long enough, she might take him for dead, if he could just . . .

The terrible smothering weight suddenly lifted. He gasped, filling his starved lungs while he could.

But no second assault came. He could hear Cassandra wheezing like an asthma victim.

Escott dislodged the cushion. It dropped away, but he couldn't see Cassandra. She was over by the mummy case, panting, trying to speak to her gods. He worked the knife blade . . . quickly now, while she was . . .

Then came the awful gagging sounds, followed by a thump and thrashing.

Oh, God . . . no!

He frantically hurried to cut free.

By the time he succeeded, it was long over. Cassandra lay curled at the foot of the case, her face rounded like an apple and just as red. Her lips were distended, her swollen tongue showing between them, huge and purple. He hastily turned away and staggered upstairs.

A few days later, after he'd had enough to drink, Escott sat in his living room and told his partner what had happened.

Jack Fleming remained quiet through the whole story, moving his long lanky form only once to pour Escott another shot of gin. "Tough place to be," he said. "I don't know how you could have done things different."

Escott lifted one hand in a hopeless gesture. The red marks on his wrists were nearly faded. "I thought she would only suffer a sneezing fit, and that would buy me enough time to get free. I had no idea her allergy was so deadly."

"Is that why you wiped up all your prints and never called the cops?"

"I phoned the police, once I was well away. Couldn't just leave her there. But nothing good would come of my involvement. They can draw their own conclusions about how she died—after they're done digging up her garden. The paper said three bodies have been found so far, and they expect more to follow. Dear God."

"They couldn't have nailed you on murder one," Fleming speculated. "Involuntary manslaughter at the most."

"Self-defense, I should think."

"Self-defense? After you let that cat climb all over you?"

"The climbing all over me was the cat's idea, not mine. I just went along with it." Escott fell silent, thankful he made the delivery in Cassandra's name, not his own. With any luck he would remain forever anonymous.

Fleming picked up a book next to Escott's chair. "Reading up on Egypt? Haven't you had enough of it?"

Escott shrugged. "Knowledge is power. Perhaps if I'd known more I could have talked the woman out of her twisted ceremony. She had an extraordinary talent. Gone now."

"Learn anything?"

"Nothing relevant to what I went through. I think Miss Selk made up most of it to fit her delusion. However, that cat, the way it took to me . . . I can't help but think the influence of Bast was indeed involved in some way, and that she used me to stop her erstwhile and misguided priestess. Either Bast or some other goddess."

Fleming flipped through the book, stopping on a page. "You underlined this name, but the picture's not a cat, but a woman with a feather. Maat? Is that how you say it?"

Escott grimaced. "Ma'at, the goddess of order and justice. What a dread and terrible lady she must be."

Cat Among the Rabbits

Edward D. Hoch

Marty Olson called his place a rabbitry and boasted that he had over two hundred does and twenty bucks on the premises. Walking down the aisle between the rows of rabbit cages, Paula Glen didn't doubt it for a moment.

"I've had good luck with the place," he told her.

"You should have, with all these rabbit's feet." Paula had been sent out by her home business magazine to do a feature story on the rabbitry and she hardly knew where to begin. They were in the north country of New York State, not far from the Canadian border, in an area so remote that Olson had invited her to stay the night before he drove her twenty miles west to the small Massena airport in the morning.

Olson was older than her by a couple of decades, and reminded her of a farmer uncle her family had visited every summer, taking pride in touring the cow barn with his visitors. "These are my dwarf rabbits in this section," he pointed out. "Mini Lops, Netherland Dwarfs, a Mini Rex. As we go down the line they get bigger. Here are some New Zealand Whites and Silver Giants, a Flemish Giant and a few Rhinelanders. I'll bet this is one you've never seen." He'd paused before a good-sized one that looked somehow out of place among the others. "It's a Swamp Rabbit, not as cuddly as some."

But the creature in the bottom cage, near the floor, took her attention. "This one looks like a cat!"

Marty Olson chuckled. "It is a cat! That's Homer."

"What's he doing in a rabbit cage?"

"Homer has the run of the place. Sometimes if he finds an empty cage with the door open he climbs inside."

Paula bent to look more closely. Homer was a calico cat with variegated black, yellow and white markings. He seemed friendly enough and actually stuck out his paw when she offered a finger. "Do you have him to keep the rabbits in line?" she asked.

The balding man laughed. "Oh, they're pretty tame critters. But it's always good to have a cat around. I let him out to prowl every night and often he brings me back a mouse or two in the morning."

She gazed out the window at the flat grassland that extended some two hundred feet to a line of trees. "Do you ever catch wild rabbits?"

"Rarely, unless they come calling and won't go away. Most of these are pure-bred right on our premises." He opened one of the cages, pulling out a lovely Angora. "This is Buffy, one of my favorites."

"Hello, Buffy." She scratched the rabbit's ear, and then remembered she should be taking notes on all this. She reached into her shoulder bag for a notebook and pen. "How long have you had the rabbitry?"

"My wife and I bought it eight years ago. Wasn't much at the time, but we added this whole rear section and doubled the number of rabbit cages."

"Will I get to meet your wife?"

"Julie? Sure. She's a teacher in town but she'll be along soon."

"Do you have any help with this? Children or neighbors?"

He smiled. "I have a grown son by my first marriage but

he's on the West Coast. There's just Julie and me, but I do most of the work with the bunnies. She takes care of the bookkeeping."

They left the rabbitry by the back door and strolled across the grass.

Over near the trees was a large shed with a riding mower and other gardening equipment. "The Canadian border's only a mile away," he told her, gesturing through the trees. "Sometimes we have trouble with illegal aliens, especially now that security's been tightened because of the terrorism."

"I'll bet you get some cold winters up here."

"Oh, sure. And lots of snow. It's good you came in June."

Olson's rabbitry was connected to their house through a door off the kitchen, but he led her in through a side door and seated her comfortably in the family room while he summarized the successes and failures of his home business. Paula had filled three pages with notes by the time Julie Olson arrived home from school. She was attractive and much younger than her husband, not unusual for a second marriage. She wore her dark hair in a tousled look similar to Paula's own, and Paula guessed they were about the same age, close to thirty.

After Olson made the introductions Julie smiled and said, "I can't imagine anyone flying up here from New York just to see our rabbits."

"The magazine covers all sorts of home businesses," Paula explained. "But running a rabbitry was a new one on us and we decided it was worth a story, maybe even a cover if I can get any decent pictures with this digital camera."

"Did Marty tell you about the time that Precious got out of her cage and hid for two days? We were goofy searching everywhere for her. We finally found her behind the freezer in the kitchen."

"Do you have names for all your rabbits?"

"About thirty of the favorites," Olson replied. "We add names from time to time if they show some distinctive traits. A tough one that fights a lot we call Rambo."

"I'll have to see that one."

Julie sat down on the sofa opposite them and Homer immediately appeared from somewhere to hop onto her lap. She smiled and stroked his fur. "We're a little family here. A big family, if you count the rabbits."

"Homer is a lovely cat."

"He's a big baby. Any sharp sound will throw him into a panic. On the Fourth of July and during hunting season we just have to keep him in the house. Otherwise he's a nervous wreck for days. I suppose if he lived in New York he'd get used to the noise quickly enough."

"Your husband says there's pretty good money in breeding and selling rabbits."

"Oh, sure. Pet shops love them. We could make even more selling them to pharmaceutical labs for testing but that's too cruel. I won't allow it."

"What grades do you teach?" I asked her.

"Ninth grade general science. I enjoy it. And we can use the money. The rabbit business is full of hops and skips."

"That reminds me," Olson said. "The UPS guy didn't bring the shipment of rabbit pellets I ordered. I'll have to run into town and pick up enough to tide us over. Want to come along?"

She shook her head. "Let me check our e-mail for orders and then I'll start getting dinner ready."

"It's so good of you to put me up for the night," Paula

told them. "Getting in and out of here by plane is next to impossible."

"It's our pleasure," Julie said. "You might find traveling by train or bus to be easier in the long run. How about dinner? You do eat meat, don't you?"

"As long as it's not rabbit."

Olson suggested that Paula ride along with him into town and she readily agreed. Standing around watching someone else prepare dinner was always embarrassing for her, and her own kitchen skills were so minimal she hated to volunteer any help. She climbed into the passenger seat of his red pickup truck and they took off down the bumpy country road. The road was covered with red shale that raised a cloud of dust behind them. It looked like someone had bled on it.

The town was named Crawford and consisted pretty much of a firehouse, a general store, a hardware store, two churches and a gas station. He parked across from the hardware store, a fairly large place selling everything from cat, dog and rabbit food to guns and ammo. "Everything but human food," Olson explained as they entered. "Sam has an agreement with the general store lady."

Sam Whitestone was a slender, handsome man in his thirties who moved with an almost fluid motion. "Hello, Marty," he said, rising from his computer as they entered. "Who's this?"

"Miss Paula Glen from New York. She's here doing a magazine story on my rabbitry."

"No kidding!" he shifted his gaze to Paula, taking her in from head to toe, with a moment's pause at her hips. She decided that even this far north he was a New York kind of bachelor.

"I need a couple sacks of rabbit pellets, Sam, to tide me over till the UPS gets here with my monthly order."

"Sure thing. Will two be enough?"

Olson thought for a moment. "Better make it three and put it on my account."

Paula picked up one of the sacks while Olson took the other two. The phone was ringing and Whitestone grabbed it with his right hand while he wrote up the invoice with his left. "That's it," he told them. "Say hello to Julie for me."

"Will do," Olson said and Paula followed him out to the car.

"Seems like a friendly sort," she said.

"He's friendly, all right. Especially to young women."

"I gathered that."

When they arrived back at Olson's house and the rabbitry, Julie was just finishing the dinner preparations. "Sam said hello," he told her as he deposited the bags of rabbit pellets by the door to the rabbitry.

"Did you enjoy your visit to our town?" Julie asked Paula.

"Well, I have to say it's quite different from New York. Except for Sam Whitestone, that is. He reminds me of the guys you meet in bars on Third Avenue."

After dinner she sat down with both of them and gathered more material for her article. "Tell her about that time with the bear," Julie urged, and her husband launched into a long story about a bear that had come up to the house early one morning and actually broken a window of the rabbitry before he was frightened off by a couple of shots from Marty's rifle. "Homer was still outside and the shots frightened him so much he ran off and hid. It took us all day to find him."

After a few more stories Paula decided she had enough.

"But I still need some pictures." She took out her digital camera and shot several photos of the rabbitry, then a few of Olson and his wife, together and separately, doing their chores around the cages. "Let's have you holding one of the rabbits, Julie," she suggested.

"I'll get Rusty," Olson suggested. "Julie doesn't like some of the friskier ones."

Rusty posed in her arms as if he'd been doing it all his life, and Paula shot four quick poses. Then she suggested a picture of Julie holding Homer, "even though he's not a rabbit." She shot a couple and promised, "I'll send you prints of these."

With her job more or less finished for the night, Paula accepted their offer of a brandy and settled down to relax. When it got to be after eleven she decided it was time for bed. "I'll have to be up early for my plane."

"It doesn't take long but we should leave here a little after eight," Olson decided.

"I'll have breakfast on the table by seven," Julie promised.

Paula fell asleep quickly in the guest room's big feather bed. There were old lace curtains on the windows and when she opened her eyes she could see the nearly full moon shining through them. Something had awakened her, and she realized at once it was Marty Olson whispering her name.

"Paula, could you come down with me? There's a prowler out by the garden shed and I don't want to wake Julie."

She slipped on her robe and followed him into the hall, nearly tripping over Homer. As her eyes became accustomed to the dim light she realized Olson was carrying his rifle. "Is it the bear again?" she asked softly.

"Either that or someone who sneaked across the border. He may be looking for something to steal."

"What do you want me to do?" Paula asked a bit uncertainly.

"Just stay in the kitchen and watch. If anything goes wrong, dial 911." He gripped the rifle tighter and opened the side door. Paula looked out over his shoulder but could see nothing. The glowing kitchen clock showed the time to be 1:24.

Olson stepped out into the darkened yard with only the moonlight to guide him. He'd gone about twenty feet toward the shed when she heard him call out, "Who's there? Come out where I can see you!"

The shadows on the garden shed seemed to change and Paula thought the door had opened. There was a voice and then Olson shouted, "He's got a gun!" He fired two shots, quickly, from his rifle.

Paula picked up the phone and dialed the police. Then she saw that Olson had moved forward, carefully, and she followed him outside. By the time she caught up with him he was bending over a man's body face down in the doorway of the shed. A pistol lay on the ground by his right hand.

"He had a gun," Olson told her. "I had to shoot him."

From the house there came a scream as Julie broke from the side door and ran over to them. "Marty, what have you done?"

"I saw a prowler at the shed and got my rifle. When I called to him to come out I saw him point a gun at me. I had to fire in self-defense."

They didn't have to turn the body over. Julie simply stared at it and said, her voice breaking, "You've killed Sam Whitestone from the hardware store!"

★ ★ ★ ★ ★

The state police were there within ten minutes, and soon a plainclothes detective from the state CID joined the officers. His name was Wayne Rummerman, a handsome fortyish man running a bit overweight. His sleepy eyes made it appear that this accidental killing had awakened him needlessly.

"Do either of you have any idea what might have brought Mr. Whitestone out here in the middle of the night?" he asked the Olsons.

"I don't want to think about it," Marty Olson answered. "He brought a gun with him, and he meant to use it."

"You know that's not true," his wife insisted. "My God, I think you deliberately killed him!"

"Hold up here!" the detective told them. He turned to Paula. "Where do you fit into this?"

She told him the reason for her visit and even showed him the notes she'd been making. "Did you know the dead man?"

"As a matter of fact I met him yesterday afternoon for about five minutes. Mr. Olson and I drove into town for some rabbit food."

Rummerman turned back to the Olsons. "Was there trouble with Mr. Whitestone in the past, any reason why he'd come out here with a gun?"

"Nothing," Marty Olson told him. "We were the best of friends."

Julie seemed on the verge of adding something but then changed her mind.

"I'd like all of you to come down to the barracks in the morning and make statements for the record."

"I have to catch a plane for New York," Paula protested.

"Sorry, Miss. I'll have to ask you to take a later flight."

She stood by the side door watching the investigators take pictures of the body and the shed, wondering what she'd gotten herself into.

Paula slept very little the rest of the night, and when she heard Julie moving around in the kitchen she got up to join her. "I'm so sorry this had to happen while you were here," she told Paula. "I don't know what came over Marty to shoot him like that."

"I'm sure it was an accident. He thought it was someone slipping across the border."

Homer had appeared from somewhere and was rubbing against Julie's leg as she cracked some eggs into the frying pan. "I wish I could believe that," she said with a sigh.

"What do you mean?"

"Marty got upset once in a while about Sam. You saw how the guy was, always checking out the ladies. Marty thought there was something between us."

"Was there?"

She shrugged. "Nothing serious, nothing for Marty to worry about. But I couldn't convince him of that."

Paula sat down at the table and the cat shifted his attention to her. "Do you have any idea why he came here last night? Was it to see you?"

"I swear I don't know why he came."

"Had he ever come here before?"

She hesitated, and then admitted, "Once or twice when Marty was away on business. He knew it was pretty lonely out here and he checked to see that I was okay."

They heard Marty descending the stairs and shifted the conversation to the weather. "Are the winters bad here?" Paula asked.

"Oh, we survive. The rabbits love the snow. Sometimes

we think we should turn them loose in it, but they probably wouldn't come back."

Her husband was quiet through breakfast and said very little on the drive to the state police barracks. Paula was aware that Julie made little effort at conversation herself. Before they left the house Paula had phoned her New York office to tell them she wouldn't be in that afternoon as planned.

Wayne Rummerman proved to be a detective sergeant in the criminal investigation division, and he greeted them at his office door. "I'll need to take your statements individually," he told them. "I'd like to start with Miss Glen here, so she can be on her way back to New York."

Paula followed him into the little office and took a seat in the chair he'd indicated. "Now what can you tell me about this matter, Miss Glen? It is Miss, isn't it?"

"That's right."

"And you're a magazine writer?"

"Yes."

"I suppose there are a great many unmarried career women in New York."

"Is that a question?"

"Excuse me, I'm not trying to pry into your personal life. I've been a bit lonely since my wife died, and sometimes I think lonely people can recognize each other. Just tell me what you know about this matter."

She described the previous day's events in detail, as well as she could remember them. When she finished, he asked, "Was there any hint of an affair between Mrs. Olson and the dead man?"

Paula remembered what Julie had told her at breakfast, but answered, "I have no way of knowing that. I only met these people yesterday."

Rummerman glanced at the papers on his desk. "The gun Whitestone had wasn't registered to him, but he sold them at the store. He could have taken it out of his stock. He might have gone out there to see Julie Olson and taken it along for protection."

"Or everything Marty Olson says might be true. He heard someone prowling around the shed and went out there with his rifle. The man had a gun and Olson fired first."

The detective smiled slightly. "Do you believe that?"

"I believe what I saw."

He asked her a few more questions and then had her wait while he talked to the others. Julie went in next, leaving Paula on the bench with Olson.

"What did he want to know?" Marty asked.

"Just what I saw. I told him everything I could remember."

Olson nodded sadly. "It was a terrible accident. I hope they're not trying to make something else out of it."

Julie came out presently and her husband went in for his session. To pass the time Paula took the digital camera from her purse and reviewed the pictures she'd shot the day before.

"This one of you and Homer is good," she said, showing it to Julie. "I probably can't find an excuse to run it in a story about the rabbitry, though."

She looked at some of the others but kept coming back to Homer.

"You know something—"

"What?" Julie asked.

"I have to ask you this and I hope you'll answer me truthfully."

"Go ahead."

Edward D. Hoch

"Were you expecting Sam to come out there last night?"

"No! He would never come out when Marty was home."

"Unless he thought you needed him."

She looked puzzled. "What are you talking about?"

Sergeant Rummerman came out then with Marty. "I think that'll be all for now. Thank you for coming in."

"There's one thing I just thought of," Paula said, and the words seemed to be coming out of someone else. They all stared at her.

"What's that?" Rummerman asked.

She took a deep breath. "The curious incident of the cat in the night-time."

"The cat did nothing in the night-time," Marty Olson said.

"That was the curious incident. You told me yourself that you let Homer out every night and he sometimes came back in the morning with a dead mouse or two."

"Yes," he said softly.

"You didn't let him out last night. I almost tripped over him when I left my room to follow you downstairs."

"I—"

"You didn't let him out because he ran away and hid when he heard fireworks or gunshots. And you knew there'd be gunshots. The only way you could have known that was if you'd lured Sam Whitestone out there to kill him."

"That's crazy! How could I have lured him out?"

"Perhaps by sending an urgent e-mail supposedly from your wife. My visit was your perfect opportunity. You needed a witness to back up your story and it couldn't be Julie. She might have recognized Whitestone, even at night, and kept you from firing."

"The man had a gun," Olson reminded her.

"Only the one that you dropped by his hand when you bent over the body. I just met the man for a few minutes

94

but it was long enough to know he was left-handed. In your haste you dropped the gun by his right hand."

His face clouded with anger and he would have hit her if Sergeant Rummerman hadn't grabbed his arm.

Paula phoned her editor in New York and explained what had happened.

"You're telling me that the subject of your article has been arrested for murder?" he asked, not certain he'd heard her correctly.

"That's right."

"Well, that kills the story. We can't do a piece on his rabbitry if he's in jail charged with murder, especially not if our feature writer helped put him there."

"I only—"

"When will you be back?"

"I just missed the last plane. I think my best bet now is a bus to Plattsburgh. I can get a train to New York from there and be home by midnight."

"All right," he said generously. "Take the morning off."

When Julie drove her to the bus station she had a surprise. It was Homer in a carrying case, ready to travel. "I want you to have him," she said. "You did a lot for me, and I don't even know if I can handle all those rabbits alone. I couldn't handle Homer too. I think he's sort of a New York animal anyway."

"Well, thank you," Paula told her, meaning it. "Maybe a year from now I'll come back and do a story on your rabbitry."

"If I'm still in business."

While she waited for the bus she phoned the state police barracks and spoke to Sergeant Rummerman. "Is this Miss Sherlock?" he asked.

She laughed and asked, "Will I have to return here for the trial?"

"Too soon to tell. The District Attorney may be willing to accept a guilty plea to manslaughter. I have your phone number in Manhattan. I'll let you know how things work out."

"I'd appreciate that."

"Paula?" It was the first time he'd used her given name.

"Yes?"

"Sometimes I have to go to New York on business. Maybe we could have dinner together."

"I'd like that," she said.

Her bus had pulled in. She picked up the cat carrier and her overnight bag, hurrying to get on.

Paw-trait of a Murderer

John Helfers

The man's body was sitting cross-legged on a woven *tatami* mat in the middle of the room. His chin was resting on his chest, and his eyes were closed. An ink brush rested in his open right hand, a writing stone was held loosely in his left. On the floor before him lay a pristine scroll of rice paper.

From what Kitsune could see, it looked like the man was sleeping. Only when he walked around the still form did he see the dark stain on the man's kimono, his blood dripping down to pool with the ink from the spilled pot beside him. A line of strange markings near the ink puddle caught his eye, but before he could examine them further, a voice commanded his full attention.

"Kitsune! Do not touch anything!"

Straightening, the boy turned back to the doorway, where the vaguely middle-aged man who had spoken to him was talking with the captain of the house guards. Kitsune edged closer and picked up the conversation in mid-sentence.

"—you realize the delicacy of the situation, Ashiga-sama. With the generals of Clan Yoshitsune assembled, I don't know how long we can keep the death of the *daimyo* quiet. If they find out, they will immediately begin arguing as to who should take over the province. If the rights of power are not legally and quickly handed down, it could lead to civil war, which we cannot afford, not with enemies surrounding us," the captain said.

"It is not the enemies outside your province I would be concerned with, but the enemies within," the older man replied. "What of Yoshitsune's son? Surely a suitable governor can rule the province until he is of a proper age."

"That's just it, there are too many generals who would see the *daimyo*'s death as a means to gain control. Once installed, the boy would have an 'accident' and the acting governor could take over," the house captain said, frowning. "Some wouldn't even be that sly about it, they would just use their troops to take over the castle."

"That would be inconvenient," the older man said. "Spread the word that the *daimyo* is ill and must rest for the next twenty-four hours with no visitors, on my orders. Post only guards you trust around the boy day and night, and no one is to see him unless you have cleared the visit personally. I will see what I can do. Please leave so I may examine the scene here. My associate outside will make sure we are not disturbed."

"Should the boy be here?" the captain asked. "It might disturb him to be in the presence of . . ." he motioned towards the body.

"I have every confidence in my retainer's ability to conduct himself in the proper manner. Besides," the man said with a small grin, "he's probably seen things that would disturb *you*. Go now."

The captain of the guards bowed deeply, turned, and strode out of the room. As he slid the paper and wood door aside, Kitsune saw the familiar form of Maseda, his mentor's samurai bodyguard, standing just to the left of the door. He smiled, then quickly turned back to the older man.

"If you are done eavesdropping on conversations that do not concern you, perhaps you would care to tell me what you have observed so far," the man said.

Kitsune gulped and stepped forward, taking a close look at the body. Now that he was able to study it, the dead man's face wore an expression of calm, not fear, pain, or anger as he had expected. "There is a peaceful look about him, and the brush in his hand is undamaged. Therefore he must have died instantly. Only a samurai or a ninja would know how to kill so cleanly."

The older man nodded. "Very good. What else?"

Kitsune thought for a moment. "The fact that he was relaxed when attacked indicates he was taken by surprise." He looked up at the roof, which was composed of wooden panels that could be opened to let the sun in. "I would examine the roof for signs of someone letting himself in that way, perhaps climbing down on a rope, stabbing Yoshitsune, then climbing back up."

"Perhaps," the older man's expression was unreadable, as usual. "More?"

Kitsune walked around the body, pausing when he got to the pool of ink. He bent down to study the strange marks he saw earlier, then looked up at his mentor. "Yoshitsune-sama was not alone." He pointed to the black paw prints that were tracked across the otherwise spotless white floor. "His cat was with him, and escaped either when the assassin fled or when the serving girl discovered the body," Kitsune said.

Asano nodded once. "So, based on what you have observed, how would you begin your investigation?"

Kitsune thought for a few minutes before answering. "I would probably question the serving girl to see if she saw anything, then take statements from everyone on the grounds to see where they were at the time of the attack. I would compare the statements to see who was alone or closest to the *daimyo*'s room and try to find a weakness in those individuals' alibis, thereby hopefully eliciting a confession."

Asano nodded again, more thoughtfully this time. "A sound plan, but aren't you forgetting one thing?"

Kitsune frowned, retracing his plan in his head. "I don't believe so."

"Actually, there are two things. First, the fact that Yoshitsune-sama died cleanly may not only indicate that he was taken by surprise, but that he knew his attacker. One of the generals may have thought that, with all of the commanding officers attending the council, now would be the perfect time to remove his obstacle to taking power, and perhaps even throw suspicion on one of the others. What you will be doing this afternoon is finding out which of Yoshitsune's military leaders was alone at the time of his death."

"How can you be sure it was one of them?" Kitsune asked.

"Because of the killing blow," Asano replied. "As you said, only a samurai or a ninja would know how to strike so cleanly. And, if I know the generals, none of them would trust anyone else to take care of this matter."

"And what will you be doing?" Kitsune asked.

Asano smiled. "I will be interviewing the witness."

"What witness?" Kitsune asked.

"Why, the cat, of course," Asano replied.

Later that afternoon, Kitsune trotted back into the castle, searching for Asano. He went to the room where the body was and saw Maseda guarding the door, still as a statue.

Kitsune went up to him. "Has Asano returned here today?"

Maseda shook his head, pointed down the corridor, and held up three fingers. Kitsune bowed, turned, and started down the hall. Three rooms down, Maseda had told him. At the third sliding panel, he tapped gently on the wooden frame.

"Enter," Asano's voice came from within. Kitsune pushed the panel open and stepped inside.

Compared to the orderly neatness of the other rooms, with their soft white paper walls, polished wooden beams, and swept floors, this area was a mess. Several pots of paint were scattered around the floor. Dozens of sheets of valuable rice paper were hung on every wall at varying heights, none more than a foot off the ground. These were smeared with paint in dizzying combinations, from multi-colored bursts of red, blue, and green to delicate patterns that resembled flowers or ornate gardens. Multi-colored paw prints were everywhere, tracked around the room until it was impossible to tell where one set ended and another began.

In the middle of it all sat Asano, stroking a black Persian resting on his lap. When Kitsune entered the man and cat both looked up at him at the exact same time. Kitsune shivered involuntarily as he approached, bowed, and sat down.

"What news?" Asano asked, his own slitted black eyes remarkably cat-like in the gloom.

"Three generals were alone at the time Yoshitsune was killed. General Konami, who leads the Crane regiment, was walking in the garden. General Ryuga, leader of the Tiger regiment, was writing a letter in his quarters. General Tokushu, commander of the Lotus regiment, was riding his stallion," Kitsune said.

"Interesting. Did Ryuga-sama say whom the letter was for?"

"He claimed he was writing to his wife," Kitsune said.

Asano nodded. "Did Tokushu-sama have the stable boy get his horse, or did he have it out already?"

"The stable boy said that Tokushu-sama had taken his horse out that morning, and returned it just a few minutes before I came to see him. In fact, he was rubbing it down as we talked."

"Did the horse look winded?" Asano asked.

"Yes, he was sweaty and lathered, as if he had been ridden hard," Kitsune replied.

"Hm. Any one of them could have easily killed the *daimyo*. While you were out, I was having a most illuminating conversation with Ningpo-san," Asano said. When he didn't say anything more, Kitsune's eyes dropped to the cat, who stared back at him unruffled.

"And?" Kitsune asked.

"She knows who the murderer is," Asano said.

"Great, then all we have to do is assemble everyone who was on the castle grounds, and have her point him or her out. Surely her negative reaction will be enough for a trial," Kitsune said.

"No, Kitsune, you do not understand. I know she witnessed what happened in Yoshitsune's room, however, she does not realize what she has seen. If we were to attempt your test, then Ningpo-san might seize on the aura of someone that cats naturally find repellent, and could condemn an innocent man to death. No, there is another way to uncover the killer, and the cat is the key," Asano said.

"But if the cat can't tell you who did it, why don't you just contact the spirits and ask them who killed the *daimyo*? Surely they saw it happen," Kitsune said.

Asano shook his head. "Pah, their assistance is not required for this minor matter. If one goes to the spirits too much, then they begin to believe that one relies on them for everything, which can lead to all sorts of difficulty. Better to exercise the mind and solve this using more earthly methods."

"But how are we to accomplish that?" Kitsune asked.

"That is my business," Asano said. "I will need plenty of clean rice paper and pots of paint in every color you can find. By tomorrow morning, we shall have our murderer."

The next morning dawned clear and bright. Kitsune rose to watch the sunrise and meditate, then went to Asano's room. He'd spent the previous evening hanging the sheets of rice paper and leaving the pots of paint on the floor of the cat's playroom as instructed.

Maseda was standing outside Asano's quarters. He opened the door for Kitsune, and motioned him inside. Asano was sitting in the lotus position, his eyes closed.

"Asano?" Kitsune asked, bowing.

Asano's eyes opened and the old-not old man regarded him. "It is time. Have the captain of the guard summon the three generals and bring them to the room we were in last night."

Kitsune bowed and ran to find Captain Ikama. He located him in the main courtyard and gave him Asano's message, then ran back to find Asano sitting in the middle of the cat-tracked floor in the paint room. The cat Ningpo, her paws streaked with several colors of paint, still rested on his lap, smiling her peculiar smile. Maseda, looking as inconspicuous as ever, stood quietly in a corner of the room. Kitsune bowed again and waited beside the door. He noticed that only one sheet of rice paper now hung on the wall to the left of the entrance.

A few minutes later, Kitsune heard the sounds of men

walking and talking amongst themselves as they came down the hallway. Captain Ikama entered, bowed to Asano, and walked over to him, where the two men whispered for a few moments. He then moved to stand on the other side of the door. Then the three generals came in, all dressed in kimonos with *katanas* by their sides. Each of their kimonos was decorated on the front, back, and sleeves with patterns representing their regiments. General Konami was tall and thin, with a long nose much like his unit's namesake. His kimono was covered with the image of a crane spreading its wings to fly. General Ryugu was short but thickly muscled, with his hair cropped close to his head, and a long scar that wound its way down one cheek. His orange and black robe was decorated with dozens of sitting tigers. General Tokushu, commander of the Lotus regiment, was a handsome man in an immaculately pressed silk kimono covered in lotus blossoms. Of the three men, he seemed the most annoyed at being summoned here.

"Honored gentlemen, once again I humbly thank you for meeting us here on such short notice," Captain Ikama began. "It is my sad duty to inform you that our *daimyo*, Lord Yoshitsune Iretsu, died yesterday." The captain paused to let the news sink in. "He was murdered, killed by a single *katana* thrust to the heart."

The generals murmured among themselves. Then General Ryugu stepped forward, bowing slightly. "It is indeed a most sorrowful matter. But what does this have to do with us?" he asked, the other two nodding in confused agreement.

"For that answer, I will turn to the physician of the Royal Court of his Most Revered Emperor Yamata, Master Ashiga Asano." Captain Ikama bowed to Asano, who had not moved, but still sat in the center of the room, his nimble fingers stroking the cat in his lap.

"Honored gentlemen, the captain of the guard has asked me, a humble physician, to investigate this terrible matter. After doing so, I have come to the conclusion that one of you three had both motive and opportunity to commit this most dishonorable crime," Asano said.

The three generals exchanged suspicious glances with each other.

"What the murderer did not count on was that a witness saw this horrible deed," Asano continued. "That witness is sitting on my lap as I speak."

All eyes went to the black Persian cat lounging on Asano's lap.

General Konami was the first to break the silence. "This is ridiculous. How will a cat tell us who may have killed Lord Yoshitsune?"

"Regardless, this cat has told me who killed Lord Yoshitsune. The proof is hanging on the wall there," Asano said, motioning.

The three generals, Asano, Kitsune, and the captain of the guard turned towards the wall where the lone sheet of rice paper hung. On it was what looked like rough brush strokes in the shape of a man dressed in a kimono and carrying a *katana*. The robe in the painting was covered with paw prints that decorated the sleeves and front.

"What the murderer didn't know is that Yoshitsune's cat Ningpo-san is one of the rare breed of painting cats," Asano said. "When left here with paper and paint, she produced this rather accurate picture of the murderer."

Kitsune saw the eyes of the generals widen as they studied the painting. Asano continued as if he hadn't noticed. "As you can see by the design on the kimono, it is obvious which one is guilty."

For an instant, no one moved. Then the steel hiss of a *katana* being drawn split the silence. Kitsune looked back in time to see one of the generals leaping towards Asano, his blade raised above his head to split the sitting man in two with one stroke. Just as he was about to bring the sword down, Maseda appeared behind Asano, his own *katana* blocking the other man's and sending it spinning off into a corner of the room. Just as quickly, Maseda's blade was at the man's throat, followed by the other two generals, and Captain Ikama's swords.

"General Tokushu, I hereby arrest you on the charge of murder of our Lord Yoshitsune," the captain said. "Generals Konami, Ryugu, please escort the general to a holding cell and place him under guard until his trial."

The two generals escorted the now pale Tokushu out of the room. The once proud general could be heard muttering as he left. "Demon cat . . . how could it have known?"

Once the general was gone, Captain Ikama turned to Asano. "How did the cat know indeed?"

"Well, the cat was indeed part of the solution, but not the entire solution," Asano said. "When I saw that Ningposan was a painting cat, I realized how I could trap the murderer.

"To be fair, Ningpo is possessed of uncommon skill. I simply left her in here with rice paper and paint, and she supplied me with several paintings. It was then a simple matter of selecting the one that most closely resembled a samurai and making a few artistic additions to strengthen the image. In particular, I added the paw prints, knowing that that would be the final touch that would unmask the villain."

"But how did the paw prints make the difference?" Kitsune asked.

"That was the crucial element for all three men," Asano replied. "Once I found out which regiments the three generals belonged to, I selected the paw print of the cat for the kimono marking because each of the men would identify with it."

"I believe I see what you mean," Captain Ikama said. "Tokushu-sama would see the prints as the marking of the lotus, Konami-sama would interpret them as a crane unfurling its wings to fly—"

"—and Ryugu-sama would see a tiger sitting on its haunches, each one the symbol of their regiment. The killer would think the cat had marked him as guilty—" Kitsune said.

"—and betray himself, although I thought the criminal would try to flee rather than kill the only witness," Asano said.

"You mean Tokushu-sama was trying to kill the cat?" the captain asked.

"Well, both of us actually," Asano said. "That was why I was holding Ningpo-san on my lap, to present a more tempting target."

"Amazing," Captain Ikama said. "But what of the province? Who will run it now?"

"I think the best way to handle the question of which general will be governor until Yoshitsune's son becomes of age would be to make none of the generals governor. Rather, I will draw up a formal decree, backed by the Imperial Palace, that will make you, Captain Ikama, governor of this province until the boy is of ruling age. I trust this will be suitable?" Asano asked with a smile.

Captain Ikama could only nod at this most heavenly turn of events. And Ningpo, still sitting on Asano's lap, smiled her inscrutable smile, looking for all the world as if the events of that day had unfolded just as she had wished.

The Smile of a Cat

Brendan DuBois

So it had finally come down to this, everything planned, GMC van purchased and prepared for his upcoming adventures, bank account drained and enough cash for at least six months of . . . well, fun. That's right, he thought, getting ready to leave the home he had just burglarized. Fun. After years of work and planning, he was getting ready to hit the open road and do what he always—deep down—knew what he had been born to do. He wasn't sure what little twist in genetics, some little fault in his upbringing, had brought him to this, and he really didn't care that much. All he cared now was to wrap things up and get going.

In the clean kitchen he looked around, one last time. The woman who owned this house had been dead for three days, but he had nothing to do with her death. Nope. Can't pin this on me. Not yet, he thought, smiling, as he picked up the small laundry bag with the jewelry, coins, and cash he had found. Nope, not yet. Right now he had not crossed that big thick line, but for the past year, he had been working a sweet little deal, criss-crossing the great American heartland. He went into small towns and cities, bought local newspapers, read the obituaries of the recently deceased, and when family and friends were at the church, singing praises and hymns to the memory of the dear departed, he'd been in their home or apartment or condo, working quickly to strip stuff that could be easily fenced for cash.

Not a bad scam at all, and this would be the last one for the foreseeable future. For he was tired of doing the work, tired of robbing empty residences. No, the next step was going to be bloodier, was going to be juicier. And he could hardly wait. It had been a long drought of dreams, planning and fantasies, and now . . . well, so long, Kansas.

He stepped out the rear kitchen door, and nearly tripped over something. He jumped down to the small rear lawn, looked back in the late afternoon light to see what had nearly fouled him up. He almost laughed. A cat. A short-haired, black and white cat, who was sitting on the steps, staring at him. The cat looked clean and well-groomed, and strangely enough, its left paw and leg were a light gray.

"Good going, guy," he said. "Nearly caused me to break my neck."

The cat stayed there, staring at him patiently. He remembered growing up in a small town in upstate New York, how he had a cat just like this. Black and white. Roscoe. That had been his name. Lived a long time and was a sassy guy, who enjoyed sitting up by his head when he was sleeping. Roscoe had lived until he had been away in a state facility, serving some juvie time, and he got sick and had to be put down. Never forgave Mom and Dad for doing that without asking him first. Not ever.

He went to the van, unlocked it and put his take away. Time, time to get moving, before nosey neighbors or whomever decided to come over and check him out. The side of the van was nice and clean, and had two signs—made from a magnetic strip—set on each side: GEORGE'S FLORAL DELIVERIES, followed by an 800 number. What could be more typical at a recently deceased's home, than a floral delivery van? A good cover, one that had served him well in a number of states.

He looked back at the rear yard. The cat wasn't there. So. Then, a start. Something had just rubbed at his shins. He looked down and the cat was sitting there, looking up at him.

"Hey, pal," he said. "What's up?"

Bump, bump, bump. The cat kept on rubbing up against him, and a thought came to him. He bent down and picked him up, held him and rubbed his belly. "I think I get it," he said. "That poor lady who died here, she was yours, right?"

The cat was peaceful in his arms, as he stroked the soft belly. "And you've been alone ever since she died. Hmmm."

He liked the look of the cat. It wasn't purring and didn't seem overly friendly, but the cat seemed to like being held. And what kind of future would the cat have? He felt around the collar, found a tiny metal nametag. OREO. Like the black and white cookies, and one of his favorite snacks.

He rubbed his face on Oreo's fur. "Poor guy," he said. "Bet the relatives left you here all alone. Bet you're going to end up in a shelter, hunh?"

Oreo seemed to rub his furry face back around him, and that's when he decided. Right then. He opened the door and dropped Oreo on the driver's seat to his van. Time, he thought. Got to get going.

"All right, pal," he said. "Fifteen seconds. You've got fifteen seconds to make up your mind. If you're gonna stay with me, don't move. If you're gonna stay here and wait until this lady's relatives decide what to do with you, then jump out."

He started counting off in his mind, one, two, three . . . and when he reached fifteen, he got into the van. Oreo jumped over to the passenger's seat and that made him smile. It had been a long time since he had been with a cat in his arms, and he was surprised at how good he felt.

"Okay, Oreo, time to make tracks," he said, as he started up the van.

He drove for fifteen minutes, out of the tiny Kansas town, until he reached a strip of highway that was bordered on both sides by corn fields. He got out, removed the magnetic signs from both sides of the van, and put them away in the rear. He got back in and drove for another hour, and Oreo sat like a little statue, in the passenger's seat. Every now and then he reached over and rubbed the little guy's head, and he was smiling again as he found a Wal-Mart. He went in and twenty minutes later, came out with cat food (dry and moist), a cat bed, food bowl, water bowl, litter box, cat litter, catnip, and a few toys. Why not? The driving was going to be lonely and it would nice to have company, before the real fun started.

That night he stretched out in the rear of the van, in a sleeping bag over a foam mattress. Dinner had been take-out chicken, and had been pretty good. Oreo had sat in the passenger's seat, and had quietly begged, by reaching over and pawing his arm. He fed Oreo little pieces of chicken meat, and when Oreo decided he had had enough, he had sat there and gently washed his face.

Now, Oreo was sitting next to him, on a folded-over wool blanket. He shifted around so he could look at him, and rubbed his head. "There, that's not so bad, is it?"

The cat took his rubbing well, but still didn't purr. There was a tiny battery-driven lamp that illuminated the interior of the van, and he had a paperback book in his hand. But he felt like talking to the cat, as strange as that was.

"Glad you came along," he said, rubbing the head.

"Thing is, guy, it does get lonely out on the road."

The cat stayed still.

"Of course, I could do things differently. Like renting a motel room. Or a campground site. Go out to bars. But the problem with that is, you leave a record, you know? People remember you, there's credit card receipts, stuff like that. But the way I do things, paying in cash, camping out on deserted dirt roads, well, nobody knows I'm out here. Not a single person."

He moved around, opened up his paperback book. It was a true crime book, about a serial killer that had traveled across the United States, and the book promised TWELVE PAGES OF ACTUAL CRIME SCENE PHOTOS. He wondered if and when a book would ever be written about him, when the time came, and he smiled at the thought. Maybe, maybe so, but the book's author would never know his name, not ever, because he planned to be good at what he was about to do, and not get caught.

No sir, not get caught. He was about ready to start on his new path, and getting caught was definitely not on the agenda.

During the night he woke up. A dream? A noise? He opened his eyes and the light from the overhead moon lit up the van's interior. A soft touch upon his nose. Oreo, checking up on him. That's what. It made him smile. Just like Roscoe used to do, when he was a boy. The cat didn't do it because it was thirsty or hungry. No, the cat did it because it wanted to make sure that it wasn't alone.

"Hey, pal," he said, reaching out, scratching between its ears. "Just seeing if I was alive, right?"

The cat stayed still, not moving, just accepting his

touch. He moved closer to the cat and cocked an ear. Nothing. Not a sound.

"You're not purring," he said. "Why's that?"

Silence.

"I mean, Roscoe used to purr all the time. He loved to purr. How come you're not purring?"

The silence remained.

He felt himself get agitated. "I took you in, I gave you food and water and attention. If it wasn't for me, you might not even be alive. You know that? You might be in a pound, right now, ready to die. So you should purr, damn it. Purr and tell me you like it here."

He took his hand away, waited.

Oreo stared at him.

He kept waiting.

The cat reached out with a paw and touched his nose. He laughed.

"All right, you little bugger," he said, rolling back over in his sleeping bag. "You purr when you're good and ready."

By morning he was heading west, deciding it was time to leave the heartland, or whatever it was called nowadays, and he thought Colorado would be a good destination. Lots of open spaces, lots of small towns and deserted roads, and best of all, a number of good colleges. And his mouth grew dry at what was waiting for him at colleges: all those lovely, young, and naïve pretty things, waiting and waiting and waiting.

He blinked his eyes against the strong light. He turned and Oreo was sitting there on the passenger's seat, paws folded underneath him, eyes barely open. His own private little co-pilot.

"Hey there, little guy," he said, stroking the fur along his back. "Ever been to Colorado?"

The cat stayed quiet. No meows, no mewps, no purrs.

"Well, neither have I," he said. "But I tell you, we're gonna have some fun when we get there. Won't we?"

He took his hand away from the cat's back, and now held tightly onto the steering wheel.

"Oh, some serious fun."

Just before crossing over into Colorado, he found another campsite, at the end of a long dirt road that ended in a sandpit. Dinner had been a freeze-dried Army surplus meal of beef and noodles, and while it had been filling, it certainly hadn't been tasty. Even Oreo turned his nose at the bits of stringy beef he had offered him. He had changed out the little guy's litter box and now, he was back in the sleeping bag. Just for fun he laid on his back and deposited the cat on his chest, and to his surprise, Oreo remained there.

He played a little with Oreo's paws and said, "Tell you a secret?"

The cat half-closed his eyes.

"Of course I can," he said, enjoying the sensation of rubbing the pink little paw pads. "Okay, Oreo. Here's the secret of my life. No idea why, no idea how, just . . . well, I just know who I am and what I've got to do, and I can hardly wait. I mean, I've been waiting for years and years. . . ."

Oreo opened his eyes, and then, just as softly, closed them. He said, "When I was a kid, the guys in my neighborhood, they were always curious about girls. Right? I mean, why not, that's what normal boys usually find an interest in, young ladies. They stole adult magazines from stores, snuck onto certain Internet sites, and well, I went along."

Rub, rub, rub. He kept on talking. "Sure. I went along, but it did nothing for me. Nothing. I . . . I went somewhere else. That's all. Instead of stealing men's magazines, I stole true crime magazines. Instead of pictures of pretty women, I looked for pictures of car accidents or plane crashes. And instead of surfing the Internet for photos of naked college cheerleaders, I . . . I surfed the Internet, looking for crime scene and autopsy photos."

He looked at the cat. "Don't give me that look," he said. "You're a predator, just like me. And I know how cats are, and how you like to kill things. So don't give me that look."

He rubbed some more, tilted Oreo's head. "Hey," he said. "How come you don't smile?"

Oreo let his head be moved around. He looked at the cat's closed mouth, and said, "Roscoe used to smile, all the time. How come you're not smiling?"

He felt the agitation build in him again. "Daddy used to tell me that cats didn't smile. That it was just the way their head was put together. But I knew better. Roscoe was always smiling at me, and I want to know, how come you're not smiling?"

The cat's head was in his strong hands, the agitation grew and grew, and then . . . he let it go. That's all. Let it go. He raised his head and bumped his head against Oreo's.

"It's okay," he said, his voice soft. "You purr and smile when you think you have something to purr and smile about."

Something loud woke him up, a rapping noise at the rear of the van. Metal upon metal. He sat up in his sleeping bag, looked outside. A man was out there, a flashlight in hand, a man wearing—

A uniform. And a uniform cap.

Cops. Damn it, cops.

His mind raced through what was in the van, from some of the jewelry he had stolen, to the weapons secured in various places through the van, and the handcuffs, and chains. . . . Not to mention the large eyebolts fastened at various corners of the rear of the van, which he had hoped to use in a day or two.

The rapping came back, louder. "Sheriff's department, open up in there!"

If his van was searched, that's it. He'd be put away for a long time, just when he was about to start doing what he had been destined to do, just when he was about to have all those young, beautiful and defenseless women in his grasp. . . .

"Open up, or we're coming in!"

"Sure, sure," he called out, "just give me a sec!"

He scooted out of the sleeping bag, wearing just a pair of shorts. He felt around near the mattress in the semi-darkness, located a small gym bag. Unzipped. Good. Inside was a .357 Ruger revolver. If the cop out there just talked to him, fine. But if the cop wanted to search the van, then he was going to open up the van wider for the nice cop, reach into his gym bag, and then blow him into next week.

He got on his knees, undid the door, and stepped out, wincing as his bare feet hit the cold dirt. "Hey, what's going on?" he asked.

"That's what we want to know," the sheriff said, and then he felt colder. Another cop was on the other side of the van, keeping an eye on him.

Two cops. Damn it. The whole situation was getting worse and worse, and while taking down one was going to be difficult, he wasn't sure how he was going to get away with doing two.

He shivered, rubbed his arms. "Just catching some sleep, that's all, officer."

Flashlight to his eyes, blinding him. "You know this is private property?"

He shrugged. "Didn't think I was bothering anybody. Trying to save money. I'm headed out to L.A, meet up with a cousin of mine. He's got a job waiting for me."

"What kind of job?"

"Dot com. I did programming work for a place up in New York State, got dumped last month. Thought I'd travel west, see the country, and—"

The other cop—or sheriff, what did it matter—came over to the rear of the van, shaking his head. "Don't like it, Ralph. Let's roust this guy and check out his van. Just don't like it."

The first sheriff said, almost apologetically, "Sorry, pal, we're gonna want to search your van. You've got any weapons in there? Drugs?"

He shook his head. "No, sir, you go right ahead. Here, let me open the other door for you."

So he turned and reached his hand in, almost a foot to go before getting the revolver out and nailing these two meddling sheriffs, when there was movement from inside the van, and one sheriff said, "Hey, what in hell is that?"

A meow came back, and another meow. He laughed, reached in and picked up Oreo. He turned to the sheriffs and said, "It's just my bud, Oreo."

Instantly, God, it was like magic, he could sense the tension just drain away from these two characters. Standing there barefoot, in his shorts, with the cat in his arms, the two sheriffs quickly smiled and the whole atmosphere just lightened right up. The flashlights were lowered and the two guys came over, and rubbed the back of Oreo's head, scratched his belly, and made little idiot cat talk.

"What a good-looking cat you got there."

"My two kids just love our cat."

"Wish we could have one, but the missus, her allergies are something awful."

"Look at that gray paw."

That went on for a few more minutes and then, like they got their cat fix or something, the first sheriff said, "All right, you can stay the rest of the night, but get a move on in the morning, all right? There's been complaints of people trashing the area around here."

He smiled at them. "I won't leave behind a thing."

"Thanks," the second sheriff said. "You take care, now, you take care of that cat."

"You can count on it," he said, rubbing Oreo's paws. "You can count on it."

The last day of travel, he was still laughing at what happened with the two sheriffs.

"You were magic back there, simply magic," he said, driving with one hand, rubbing Oreo's head with the other. "Did you see what happened? Those two cops were ready to search the van, run a record check on me . . . spoil everything! And you stopped it!"

He laughed again, saw a sign up ahead that mentioned Boulder was only ten miles way. The mountains out here were impressive, lots of places to hide in, lots of places to hide certain people when you were done with them. . . .

Something flashed in his mind, and he looked at Oreo again. "Man, that's it. That's how it's going to happen. You're going to help me. God, that's how it's going to happen."

He rubbed the cat's head again.

"It's gonna be a piece of cake," he said, and he drove for another mile and added, "And it'd be easier if you purred. Or smiled. Can't you at least do that?"

But Oreo stayed still and quiet, just like before.

A residential street, just a ways away from the main campus of the University of Colorado. Late afternoon, just before the sun set out to the west, behind those magnificent peaks. And speaking of magnificent . . .

There she was. The very first one. Young, with long brown hair. Mid-length dungaree skirt. Short jacket. Carrying a knapsack. Were all college women issued a knapsack, or was it some kind of dress code? Not bad looking. He looked over at Oreo.

"Time to earn your keep, pal. Hold on."

He passed her and then made a U-turn further up, and then came back down the street, and he slowed and stopped and gave her his best smile. He rolled down the window and said, "Miss, excuse me?"

She stopped, alert but not unfriendly. "Yes?"

He kept on smiling. "The thing is, I'm looking for my cat."

"Really?"

"Unh-hunh."

He reached over to the passenger's side, gently picked up Oreo, and then displayed him to her. Instantly she smiled and stepped over. He went on. "The thing is, it's this guy's brother. And they're inseparable . . . well, they used to be inseparable. I had to stop a while ago, to change out a flat, and Oreo's brother ran out and I've been looking for him ever since. He's about this size, the same colors, black and white. You haven't seen him, have you?"

By now she was cooing and making kissing noises at

Oreo, scratching at the back of his head. "Ooohhh, poor little fella, missing your brother . . . that's awful."

"You know, this is being forward and all . . ."

She was still looking at the cat. "What?"

"I mean, I'm driving around, looking for Benjamin, that's Oreo's brother, and Oreo's whining and bouncing around, and getting underfoot. Would you . . . I mean, could I ask you to sit here with me, keep Oreo on your lap, while I drive and look for his brother?"

She smiled up at him. "Sure, I'll do that for the poor little guy."

And with that, she walked around the front of the van and climbed in.

Nearly an hour later, he was sweating, breathing hard. All of the planning, all of the fantasies, everything he had dreamed of for years was coming true. The young girl was in the rear of the van, spread out and handcuffed, gagged and her eyes were quite wide, tearing up, and he could only imagine what delicious thoughts were racing through her mind.

He had stripped down to his shorts again, for the air in the van had gotten thick with sweat and fear and the muffled screams of the young woman, whoever she was. He went through another gym bag, stored up forward, and smiled as he took out a long knife. There. Something fun to start with.

He made to go back to the rear of the van, where the woman was waiting for him, and Oreo was sitting there, staring at him. He looked back at the cat.

"What?" he said. "You got a problem?"

The cat just stared.

"Hey, I'm just like you, all right? Hunting the weak,

hunting the defenseless. This is what I was meant to do, and if you don't like it, you can just leave."

Oreo sat there, still.

He reached over with the knife, gently touched the top of his head. "All right, little guy. Look, thanks for bringing her in here with me. I promise to get you something nice when I'm done. Maybe tomorrow. Okay? A nice can of tuna fish or salmon."

He turned to where she was, and the thumping in his heart and head was so loud it almost hurt. Just a few seconds more, that's it. Just a few seconds more.

"Oh," he said to the cat. "One more thing. You're going to be hearing a lot of screaming in a little bit. Just ignore it, okay?"

He touched Oreo's head. "Good cat."

And sure enough, in a very short while, the interior of the van was filled with screams.

As he went back to the van, trembling, knife in his sweaty hand, Oreo made a loud, awful, hissing noise that froze him as he approached the girl.

He turned. "What the—"

And the damn cat was on him! On his face! After all he had done! After he had saved him and—

God! The pain! His eyes!

He swung out, missed, and the hissing and spitting and the howling continued.

As did the screams.

The Boulder police detective was exhausted when he got home, but smiled as he saw his wife in the living room, waiting up for him.

"Long day, hon?" she asked.

"You know it," he said, as he walked over and kissed her, and then gently touched the top of the cat's head, the new cat sitting in her lap, black and white and with a gray paw.

"How goes the investigation?" she asked.

He sat down, picked up a copy of the day's newspaper, the *Boulder Daily Camera.* "It's going," he said. "We've managed to link this guy to about a dozen or so burglaries in three other states. Combined with the kidnapping and assault of that college girl . . . well, he'll be going away for a long time. And even when he does get out, well, his eyes won't ever be the same. Don't think he could hurt anybody if he wanted to. And that girl, she was lucky, quite lucky."

His wife scratched the cat's head. "And thanks to this guy, right?"

He nodded. "Yep. The girl wasn't too clear on what happened, I mean, she was scared to death of what was going on. But just as the guy came up to her, with a knife in his hand, the cat was all over him, scratching and biting and shredding. He yelled so loud a couple of hikers came over to see what was going on . . . that cat's a hero."

His wife smiled. "That cat has a name. It's Oreo. And have you found anything out about him?"

"Yeah, he belonged to an old woman in Kansas, died a few days ago."

"Oh," his wife said. "Does . . . does the family want him back?"

He smiled at her. "No. He's here to stay, if you'd like."

"Oh, I'd like that very much."

"I had a feeling you would."

She rubbed and rubbed the cat's head, and she said, "The owner. The old lady who died. Who was she?"

He turned the front page of the newspaper. "Believe it or not, she had my job."

"Really?" his wife asked, smiling.

"Yep. One of the first woman police detectives in the whole state of Kansas. Quite famous, I guess."

His wife rubbed the cat's head and she said, "My, wouldn't your old mommy be proud of you. Hey, can you hear that? He's purring."

He put the paper down. "Purring? Hon, that sounds like an airplane engine. And he's doing something else, too."

"What's that?"

"Look closely," he said. "He's smiling."

His wife turned the head of the purring cat so she could see, and she laughed. "By God, he is. I guess he has a lot to be smiling about."

"I'm sure he does," he said, getting the strangest feeling that the cat was smiling at him, and no one else. And it seemed like a special smile, a proud smile.

Must be my imagination, he thought, and he went back to his newspaper, still listening to the loud purrs.

The Christmas Kitten

Ed Gorman

1

"She in a good mood?" I said.

The lovely and elegant Pamela Forrest looked up at me as if I'd suggested that there really *was* a Santa Claus.

"Now why would she go and do a foolish thing like that, McCain?" She smiled.

"Oh, I guess because—"

"Because it's the Christmas season, and most people are in good moods?"

"Yeah, something like that."

"Well, not our Judge Whitney."

"At least she's consistent," I said.

I had been summoned, as usual, from my law practice, where I'd been working the phones, trying to get my few clients to pay their bills. I had a 1951 Ford ragtop to support. And dreams of taking the beautiful Pamela Forrest to see the Platters concert when they were in Des Moines next month.

"You thought any more about the Platters concert?" I said.

"Oh, McCain, now why'd you have to go and bring *that* up?"

"I just thought . . ."

"You know how much I love the Platters. But I really don't think it's a good idea for the two of us to go out

124

again." She gave me a melancholy little smile. "Now I probably went and ruined your holidays and I'm sorry. You know I like you, Cody, it's just—Stew."

This was Christmas 1959 and I'd been trying since at least Christmas 1957 to get Pamela to go out with me. But we had a problem—while I loved Pamela, Pamela loved Stewart, and Stewart happened to be not only a former football star at the university but also the heir to the town's third biggest fortune.

Her intercom buzzed. "Is he out there pestering you again, Pamela?"

"No, Your Honor."

"Tell him to get his butt in here."

"Yes, Your Honor."

"And call my cousin John and tell him I'll be there around three this afternoon."

"Yes, Your Honor."

"And remind me to pick up my dry cleaning."

"Yes, Your Honor."

"And tell McCain to get his butt in here. Or did I already say that?"

"You already said that, Your Honor."

I bade goodbye to the lovely and elegant Pamela Forrest and went in to meet my master.

"You know what he did this time?" Judge Eleanor Whitney said three seconds after I crossed her threshold.

The "he" could only refer to one person in the town of Black River Falls, Iowa. And that would be our esteemed chief of police, Cliff Sykes, Jr., who has this terrible habit of arresting people for murders they didn't commit and giving Judge Whitney the pleasure of pointing out the error of his ways.

A little over a hundred years ago, Judge Whitney's family dragged a lot of money out here from the East and founded this town. They pretty much ran it until World War II, a catastrophic event that helped make Cliff Sykes, Sr., a rich and powerful man in the local wartime construction business. Sykes, Sr., used his money to put his own members on the town council, just the way the Whitneys had always done. He also started to bribe and coerce the rest of the town into doing things his way. Judge Whitney saw him as a crude outlander, of course. Where her family was conversant with Verdi, Vermeer, and Tolstoy, the Sykes family took as cultural icons Ma and Pa Kettle and Francis the Talking Mule, the same characters I go to see at the drive-in whenever possible.

Anyway, the one bit of town management the Sykes family couldn't get to was Judge Whitney's court. Every time Cliff Sykes, Jr., arrested somebody for murder, the judge called me up and put me to work. In addition to being an attorney, I'm taking extension courses in criminology. The judge thinks this qualifies me as her very own staff private investigator, so whenever she wants something looked into, she calls me. And I'm glad she does. She's my only source of steady income.

"He arrested my cousin John's son, Rick. Charged him with murdering his girlfriend. That stupid ass."

Now in a world of seven-ton crime-solving geniuses, and lady owners of investigative firms who go two hundred pounds and are as bristly as barbed wire, Judge Eleanor Whitney is actually a small, trim, and very handsome woman. And she knows how to dress herself. Today she wore a brown suede blazer, a crisp button-down, white-collar shirt, and dark fitted slacks. Inside the open collar of the shirt was a green silk scarf that complemented the green of her eyes perfectly.

She was hiked on the edge of the desk, right next to an ample supply of rubber bands.

"Sit down, McCain."

"He didn't do it."

"I said sit down. You know I hate it when you stand."

I sat down.

"He didn't do it," I said.

"Exactly. He didn't do it."

"You know, one of these times you're bound to be wrong. I mean, just by the odds, Sykes is bound to be right."

Which is what I say every time she gives me an assignment.

"Well, he isn't right this time."

Which is what she says every time I say the thing about the odds.

"His girlfriend was Linda Palmer, I take it."

"Right."

"The one found in her apartment?" She nodded.

"What's Sykes's evidence?"

"Three neighbors saw Rick running away from the apartment house the night before last."

She launched one of her rubber bands at me, thumb and forefinger style, like a pistol. She likes to see if I'll flinch when the rubber band comes within an eighth of an inch of my ear. I try never to give her that satisfaction.

"He examine Rick's car and clothes?"

"You mean fibers and blood, things like that?"

"Yeah."

She smirked. "You think Sykes would be smart enough to do something like that?"

"I guess you've got a point."

She stood up and started to pace.

You'll note that I am not permitted this luxury, standing and pacing, but for her it is fine. She is, after all, mistress of the universe.

"I just keep thinking of John. The poor guy. He's a very good man."

"I know."

"And it's going to be a pretty bleak Christmas without Rick there. I'll have to invite him out to the house."

Which was not an invitation *I* usually wanted. The judge kept a considerable number of rattlesnakes in glass cages on the first floor of her house. I was always waiting for one of them to get loose.

I stood up. "I'll get right on it." I couldn't recall ever seeing the judge in such a pensive mood. Usually, when she's going to war with Cliff Sykes, Jr., she's positively ecstatic.

But when her cousin was involved, and first cousin at that, I supposed even Judge Whitney—a woman who had buried three husbands, and who frequently golfed with President Eisenhower when he was in the Midwest, and who had been ogled by Khrushchev when he visited a nearby Iowa farm—I supposed even Judge Whitney had her melancholy moments.

She came back to her desk, perched on the edge of it, loaded up another rubber band, and shot it at me.

"Your nerves are getting better, McCain," she said. "You don't twitch as much as you used to."

"I'll take that as an example of your Christmas cheer," I said. "You noting that I don't twitch as much as I used to, I mean."

Then she glowered at me. "Nail his butt to the wall, McCain. My family's honor is at stake here. Rick's a hothead but he's not a killer. He cares too much about the family name to soil it that way."

Thus basking in the glow of Christmas spirit, not to mention a wee bit of patrician hubris, I took my leave of the handsome Judge Whitney.

2

Red Ford ragtops can get a little cold around Christmas time. I had everything buttoned down but winter winds still whacked the car every few yards or so.

The city park was filled with snowmen and Christmas angels as Bing Crosby and Perry Como and Johnny Mathis sang holiday songs over the loudspeakers lining the merchant blocks. I could remember being a kid in the holiday concerts in the park. People stood there in the glow of Christmas-tree lights listening to us sing for a good hour. I always kept warm by staring at the girl I had a crush on that particular year. Even back then, I gravitated toward the ones who didn't want me. I guess that's why my favorite holiday song is "Blue Christmas" by Elvis. It's really depressing, which gives it a certain honesty for romantics like myself.

I pulled in the drive of Linda Palmer's apartment house. It was a box with two apartments up, two down. There was a gravel parking lot in the rear. The front door was hung with holly and a plastic bust of Santa Claus.

Inside, in the vestibule area with the mailboxes, I heard Patti Page singing a Christmas song, and I got sentimental about Pamela Forrest again. During one of the times that she'd given up on good old Stewart, she'd gone out with me a few times. The dates hadn't meant much to her, but I looked back on them as the halcyon period of my entire life, when giants walked the earth and you could cut off slices of sunbeams and sell them as gold.

"Hi," I said as soon as the music was turned down and the door opened up.

The young woman who answered the bell to the apartment opposite Linda Palmer's was cute in a dungaree-doll sort of way—ponytail and Pat Boone sweatshirt and jeans rolled up to mid calf. "Hi."

"My name's McCain."

"I'm Bobbi Thomas. Aren't you Judge Whitney's assistant?"

"Well, sort of."

"So you're here about—"

"Linda Palmer."

"Poor Linda," she said, and made a sad face. "It's scary living here now. I mean, if it can happen to Linda—"

She was about to finish her sentence when two things happened at once. A tiny calico kitten came charging out of her apartment between her legs, and a tall man in a gray uniform with DERBY CLEANERS sewn on his cap walked in and handed her a package wrapped in clear plastic. Inside was a shaggy gray throw rug and a shaggy white one and a shaggy fawn-colored one.

"Appreciate your business, miss," the DERBY man said, and left.

I mostly watched the kitten. She was a sweetie. She walked straight over to the door facing Bobbi's. The card in the slot still read LINDA PALMER.

"You mind picking her up and bringing her in? I just need to put this dry cleaning away."

Ten minutes later, the three of us sat in her living room. I say three because the kitten, who'd been introduced to me

130

as Sophia, sat in my lap and sniffed my coffee cup whenever I raised it to drink. The apartment was small but nicely kept. The floors were oak and not spoiled by wall-to-wall carpeting. She took the throw rugs from the plastic dry-cleaning wrap and spread them in front of the fireplace.

"They get so dirty," she explained as she straightened the rugs, then walked over and sat down.

Then she nodded to the kitten. "We just found her downstairs in the laundry room one day. There's a small TV down there and Linda and I liked to sit down there and smoke cigarettes and drink Cokes and watch *Bandstand*. Do you think Dick Clark's a crook? My boyfriend does." She shrugged. "Ex boyfriend. We broke up." She tried again: "So do you think Dick Clark's a crook?"

A disc jockey named Alan Freed was in trouble with federal authorities for allegedly taking bribes to play certain songs on his radio show. Freed didn't have enough power to make a hit record and people felt he was being used as a scapegoat. On the other hand, Dick Clark *did* have the power to make or break a hit record (Lord, did he, with *American Bandstand* on ninety minutes several afternoons a week), but the feds had rather curiously avoided investigating him in any serious way.

"Could be," I said. "But I guess I'd rather talk about Linda."

She looked sad again. "I guess that's why I was talking about Dick Clark. So we wouldn't *have* to talk about Linda."

"I'm sorry."

She sighed. "I just have to get used to it, I guess." Then she looked at Sophia. "Isn't she sweet? We called her our Christmas kitten."

"She sure—"

"That's what I started to tell you. One day Linda and I were downstairs and there Sophia was. Just this little lost kitten. So we both sort of adopted her. We'd leave our doors open so Sophia could just wander back and forth between apartments. Sometimes she slept here, sometimes she slept over there." She raised her eyes from the kitten and looked at me. "He killed her."

"Rick?"

"Uh-huh."

"Why do you say that?"

"Why do I say that? Are you kidding? You should've seen the arguments they had."

"He ever hit her?"

"Not that I know of."

"He ever *threaten* her?"

"All the time."

"You know why?" I said.

"Because he was so jealous of her. He used to sit across the street at night and just watch her front window. He'd sit there for hours."

"Would she be in there at the time?"

"Oh, sure. He always claimed she had this big dating life on the side but she never did."

"Anything special happen lately between them?"

"You mean you don't know?"

"I guess not."

"She gave him back his engagement ring."

"And that—"

"He smashed out her bedroom window with his fist. This was in the middle of the night and he was really drunk. I called the police on him. Just because he's a Whitney doesn't mean he can break the rules anytime he feels like it."

I'd been going to ask her if she was from around here but the resentment in her voice about the Whitneys answered my question. The Whitneys had been the valley's most imperious family for a little more than a century now.

"Did the police come?"

"Sykes himself."

"And he did what?"

"Arrested him. Took him in." She gave me a significant look with her deep blue eyes. "He was relishing every minute, too. A Sykes arresting a Whitney, I mean. He was having a blast."

So then I asked her about the night of the murder. We spent twenty minutes on the subject but I didn't learn much. She'd been in her apartment all night watching TV and hadn't heard anything untoward. But when she got up to go to work in the morning and didn't hear Linda moving around in her apartment, she knocked, and, when there wasn't any answer, went in. Linda lay dead, the left side of her head smashed in, sprawled in a white bra and half-slip in front of the fireplace that was just like Bobbi's.

"Maybe I had my TV up too loud," Bobbi said. "I love westerns and it was *Gunsmoke* night. It was a good one, too. But I keep thinking that maybe if I hadn't played the TV so loud, I could've heard her—"

I shook my head. "Don't start doing that to yourself, Bobbi, or it'll never end. If only I'd done this, if only I'd done that. You did everything you could."

She sighed. "I guess you're right."

"Mind one more question?"

She shrugged and smiled. "You can see I've got a pretty busy social calendar."

"I want to try and take Rick out of the picture for a minute. Will you try?"

"You mean as a suspect?"

"Right."

"I'll try."

"All right. Now, who are three people who had something against Linda—or Rick?"

"Why Rick?"

"Because maybe the killer wanted to make it *look* as if Rick did it."

"Oh, I see." Then: "I'd have to say Gwen. Gwen Dawes. She was Rick's former girlfriend. She always blamed Linda for taking him away. You know, they hadn't been going together all that long, Rick and Linda, I mean. Gwen would still kind of pick arguments with her when she'd see them in public places."

"Gwen ever come over here and pick an argument?"

"Once, I guess."

"Remember when?"

"Couple months ago, maybe."

"What happened?"

"Nothing much. She and a couple of girlfriends were pretty drunk, and they came up on the front porch and started writing on the wall. It was juvenile stuff. Most of us graduated from high school two years ago but we're still all kids, if you see what I mean."

I wrote Gwen's name down and said, "Anybody else who bothered Linda?"

"Paul Walters, for sure."

"Paul Walters?"

"*Her* old boyfriend. He used to wait until Rick left at night and then he'd come over and pick a fight with her."

"Would she let him in?"

"Sometimes. Then there was Millie Styles. The wife of the man Linda worked for."

"Why didn't she like Linda?"

"She accused Linda of trying to steal her husband."

"Was she?"

"You had to know Linda."

"I see."

"She wasn't a rip or anything."

" 'Rip'?"

"You know, whore."

"But she—"

"—could be very flirtatious."

"More than flirtatious?"

She shrugged. "Sometimes."

"Maybe with Mr. Styles?"

"Maybe. He's an awfully handsome guy. He looks like Fabian."

She wasn't kidding. They weren't very far out of high school. That was when I felt a scratching on my chin and I looked straight down into the eager, earnest, and heartbreakingly sweet face of Sophia.

"She likes to kiss noses the way Eskimos do," Bobbi said.

We kissed noses.

Then I set Sophia down and she promptly put a paw in my coffee cup.

"Sophia!" Bobbi said. "She's always putting her paw in wet things. She's obsessed, the little devil."

Sophia paid us no attention. Tail switching, she walked across the coffee table, her left front paw leaving coffee imprints on the surface.

I stood up. "I appreciate this, Bobbi."

"You can save yourself some work."

"How would I do that?"

"There's a skating party tonight. Everybody we've talked

about is going to be there." She gave me another one of her significant looks. "Including me."

"Then I guess that's a pretty good reason to go, isn't it?" I said.

"Starts at six-thirty. It'll be very dark by then. You know how to skate?"

I smiled. "I wouldn't exactly call it skating."

"Then what would you call it?"

"Falling down is the term that comes to mind," I said.

3

Rick Whitney was even harder to love than his aunt.

"When I get out of this place, I'm going to take that hillbilly and push him off Indian Cliff."

In the past five minutes, Rick Whitney, of the long blond locks and relentlessly arrogant blue-eyed good looks, had also threatened to shoot, stab, and set fire to our beloved chief of police, Cliff Sykes, Jr. As an attorney, I wouldn't advise any of my clients to express such thoughts, especially when they were in custody, being held for premeditated murder (or as my doctor friend Stan Greenbaum likes to say, "pre-medicated murder"). "Rick, we're not getting anywhere."

He turned on me again. He'd turned on me three or four times already, pushing his face at me, jabbing his finger at me.

"Do you know what it's like for a Whitney to be in jail? Why, if my grandfather were still alive, he'd come down here and shoot Sykes right on the spot."

"Rick?"

"What?"

"Sit down and shut up."

"You're telling me to shut up?"

"Uh-huh. And to sit down."

"I don't take orders from people like you."

I stood up. "Fine. Then I'll leave."

He started to say something nasty, but just then a cloud passed over the sun and the six cells on the second floor of the police station got darker.

He said, "I'll sit down."

"And shut up?"

It was a difficult moment for a Whitney. Humility is even tougher for them than having a tooth pulled. "And shut up."

So we sat down, him on the wobbly cot across from my wobbly cot, and we talked as two drunks three cells away pretended they weren't listening to us.

"A Mrs. Mawbry who lives across the street saw you running out to your car about eleven p.m. the night of the murder. Dr. Mattingly puts the time of death at right around that time."

"She's lying."

"You know better than that."

"They just hate me because I'm a Whitney."

It's not easy going through life being of a superior species, especially when all the little people hate you for it.

"You've got fifteen seconds," I said.

"For what?"

"To stop stalling and tell me the truth. You went to the apartment and found her dead, didn't you? And then you ran away."

I watched the faces of the two eavesdropping winos. It was either stay up here in the cells, or use the room downstairs that I was sure Cliff Sykes, Jr., had bugged.

"Ten seconds."

He sighed and said, "Yeah, I found her. But I didn't kill her."

"You sure of that?"

He looked startled. "What the hell's that supposed to mean?"

"It means were you drinking that evening, and did you have any sort of alcoholic blackout? You've been known to tip a few."

"I had a couple beers earlier. That was it. No alcoholic blackout."

"All right," I said. "Now tell me the rest of it."

"Wonder if the state'll pass that new law," Chief Cliff Sykes, Jr., said to me as I was leaving the police station by the back door.

"I didn't know that you kept up on the law, Cliff, Jr."

He hated it when I added the Jr. to his name, but since he was about to do a little picking on me, I decided to do a little picking on him. With too much Brylcreem—Cliff, Jr., apparently never heard the part of the jingle that goes "A little dab'll do ya"—and his wiry moustache, he looks like a bar rat all duded up for Saturday night. He wears a khaki uniform that Warner Brothers must have rejected for an Errol Flynn western. The epaulets alone must weigh twenty-five pounds each.

"Yep, next year they're goin' to start fryin' convicts instead of hanging them."

The past few years in Iowa, we'd been debating which was the more humane way to shuffle off this mortal coil. At least when the state decides to be the shuffler and make you the shufflee.

"And I'll bet you think that Rick Whitney is going to be one of the first to sit in the electric chair, right?"

He smiled his rat smile, sucked his toothpick a little deeper into his mouth. "You said it, I didn't."

There's a saying around town that money didn't change the Sykes family any—they're still the same mean, stupid, dishonest, and uncouth people they've always been.

"Well, I hate to spoil your fun, Cliff, Jr., but he's going to be out of here by tomorrow night."

He sucked on his toothpick some more. "You and what army is gonna take him out of here?"

"Won't take an army, Cliff, Jr., I'll just find the guilty party and Rick'll walk right out of here."

He shook his head. "He thinks his piss don't stink because he's a Whitney. This time he's wrong."

4

The way I figure it, any idiot can learn to skate standing up. It takes a lot more creativity and perseverance to skate on your knees and your butt and your back.

I was putting on quite a show. Even five-year-olds were pointing at me and giggling. One of them had an adult face pasted on his tiny body. I wanted to give him the finger but I figured that probably wouldn't look quite right, me being twenty-six and an attorney and all.

Everything looked pretty tonight, gray smoke curling from the big log cabin where people hung out putting on skates and drinking hot cider and warming themselves in front of the fireplace. Christmas music played over the loudspeakers, and every few minutes you'd see a dog come skidding across the ice to meet up with its owners. Tots in snowsuits looking like Martians toddled across the ice in the wake of their parents.

The skaters seemed to come in four types: the competitive skaters who were just out tonight to hone their skills; the showoffs who kept holding their girlfriends over their heads; the lovers who were melting the ice with their scorching looks; and the junior-high kids who kept trying to knock everybody down accidentally. I guess I should add the seniors; they were the most fun to watch, all gray hair and dignity as they made their way across the ice arm in arm. They probably came here thirty or forty years ago when Model-Ts had lined the parking area, and when the music had been supplied by Rudy Vallee. They were elegant and touching to watch here on the skating rink tonight.

I stayed to the outside of the rink. I kept moving because it was at most ten above zero. Falling down kept me pretty warm, too.

I was just getting up from a spill when I saw a Levi'd leg—two Levi'd legs—standing behind me. My eyes followed the line of legs upwards and there she was. It was sort of like a dream, actually, a slightly painful one because I'd dreamt it so often and so uselessly.

There stood the beautiful and elegant Pamela Forrest. In her white woolen beret, red cable-knit sweater, and jeans, she was the embodiment of every silly and precious holiday feeling. She was even smiling.

"Well, I'm sure glad you're here," she said.

"You mean because you want to go out?"

"No, I mean because I'm glad there's somebody who's even a worse skater than I am."

"Oh," I said.

She put out a hand and helped me up. I brushed the flesh of her arm—and let my nostrils be filled with the scent of her perfume—and I got so weak momentarily I was afraid

I was going to fall right back down.

"You have a date?"

I shook my head. "Still doing some work for Judge Whitney."

She gave my arm a squeeze. "Just between you and me, McCain, I hope you solve one of these cases yourself someday."

She was referring to the fact that in every case I'd worked on, Judge Whitney always seemed to solve it just as I was starting to figure out who the actual culprit was. I had a feeling, though, that this case I'd figure out all by my lonesome.

"I don't think I've ever seen Judge Whitney as upset as she was today," I said.

"I'm worried about her. This thing with Rick, I mean. It isn't just going up against the Sykes family this time. The family honor's at stake."

I looked at her. "You have a date?"

And then she looked sad, and I knew what her answer was going to be.

"Not exactly."

"Ah. But Stewart's going to be here."

"I think so. I'm told he comes here sometimes."

"Boy, you're just as pathetic as I am."

"Well, that's a nice thing to say."

"You can't have him any more than I can have you. But neither one of us can give it up, can we?"

I took her arm and we skated. We actually did a lot better as a team than we did individually. I was going to mention that to her but I figured she would think I was just being corny and coming on to her in my usual clumsy way. If only I were as slick as Elvis in those movies of his where he sings a couple of songs and beats the crap out of every

Ed Gorman

bad guy in town, working in a few lip locks with nubile fe-
males in the interim.

I didn't recognize them at first. Their skating costumes,
so dark and tight and severe, gave them the aspect of Rus-
sian ballet artists. People whispered at them as they soared
past, and it was whispers they wanted.

David and Millie Styles were the town's "artistic fugi-
tives," as one of the purpler of the paper's writers wrote
once. Twice a year they ventured to New York to bring radical new items back to their interior decorating "salon," as
they called it, and they usually brought back a lot of even
more radical attitudes and poses. Millie had once been
quoted in the paper as saying that we should have an "All
Nude Day" twice a year in town; and David was always
standing on the library steps waving copies of banned books
in the air and demanding that they be returned to library
shelves. The thing was, I agreed with the message; it was
the messengers I didn't care for. They were wealthy, attractive dabblers who loved to outrage and shock.

In a big city, nobody would've paid them any attention.
Out here, they were celebrities.

"God, they look great, don't they?" Pamela said.

"If you like the style."

"Skin-tight, all-black skating outfits. Who else would've
thought of something like that?"

"You look a lot better."

She favored me with a forehead kiss. "Oh God, McCain,
I sure wish I could fall in love with you."

"I wish you could, too."

"But the heart has its own logic."

"That sounds familiar."

"*Peyton Place.*"

"That's right."

Peyton Place had swept through town two years ago like an army bent on destroying everything in its path. The fundamentalists not only tried to get it out of the library, they tried to ban its sale in paperback. The town literary lions, such as the Styleses, were strangely moot. They did not want to be seen defending something as plebeian as Grace Metalious's book. I was in a minority. I not only liked it, I thought it was a good book. A true one, as Hemingway often said.

On the far side of the rink, I saw David Styles skate away from his wife and head for the warming cabin.

She skated on alone.

"Excuse me. I'll be back," I said.

It took me two spills and three near-spills to reach Millie Styles.

"Evening," I said.

"Oh," she said, staring at me. "You." Apparently I looked like something her dog had just dragged in from the backyard. Something not quite dead yet.

"I wondered if we could talk."

"What in God's name would you and I have to talk about, McCain?"

"Why you killed Linda Palmer the other night."

She tried to slap me but fortunately I was going into one of my periodic dives so her slap missed me by half a foot.

I did reach out and grab her arm to steady myself, however.

"Leave me alone," she said.

"Did you find out that Linda and David were sleeping together?"

From the look in her eyes, I could see that she had. I kept thinking about what Bobbi Thomas had said, how Linda was flirtatious.

And for the first time, I felt something human for the striking if not quite pretty woman wearing too much makeup and way too many New York poses. Pain showed in her eyes. I actually felt a smidge of pity for her.

Her husband appeared magically. "Is something wrong?" Seeing the hurt in his wife's eyes, he had only scorn for me. He put a tender arm around her. "You get the hell out of here, McCain." He sounded almost paternal, he was so protective of her.

"And leave me alone," she said again, and skated away so quickly that there was no way I could possibly catch her.

Then Pamela was there again, sliding her arm through mine.

"You have to help me, McCain," she said.

"Help you what?"

"Help me look like I'm having a wonderful time."

Then I saw Stew McGinley, former college football star and idle rich boy, skating around the rink with his girlfriend, the relentlessly cheery and relentlessly gorgeous Cindy Parkhurst who had been a cheerleader at State the same year Stew was All Big-Eight.

This was the eternal triangle: I was in love with Pamela, Pamela was in love with Stew, and Stew was in love with Cindy, who not only came from the same class—right below the Whitneys—but had even more money than Stew did, and not only that but had twice done the unthinkable. She'd broken up with Stew and started dating somebody else. This was something Stew wasn't used to. *He* was supposed to do the breaking up. Stew was hooked, he was.

They were both dressed in white costumes tonight, and looked as if they would soon be on *The Ed Sullivan Show* for no other reason than simply existing.

"I guess I don't know how to do that," I said.

"How to do what?"

"How to help you look like you're having a wonderful time."

"I'm going to say something and then you throw your head back and break out laughing." She looked at me. "Ready?"

"Ready."

She said something I couldn't hear and then I threw my head back and pantomimed laughing.

I had the sense that I actually did it pretty well—after watching all those Tony Curtis movies at the drive-in, I was bound to pick up at least a few pointers about acting—but the whole thing was moot because Stew and Cindy were gazing into each other's eyes and paying no attention to us whatsoever.

"There goes my Academy Award," I said.

We tried skating again, both of us wobbling and waffling along, when I saw Paul Walters standing by the warming house smoking a cigarette. He was apparently one of those guys who didn't skate but liked to come to the rink and look at all the participants so he could feel superior to them. A sissy sport, I could hear him thinking.

"I'll be back," I said.

By the time I got to the warming house, Paul Walters had been joined by Gwen Dawes. Just as Paul was the dead girl's old boyfriend, Gwen was the suspect's old girlfriend. Those little towns in Kentucky where sisters marry brothers had nothing on our own cozy little community.

Just as I reached them, Gwen, an appealing if slightly overweight redhead, pulled Paul's face down to hers and kissed him. He kissed her right back.

"Hi," I said, as they started to separate.

They both looked at me as if I had just dropped down from a UFO.

"Oh, you're Cody McCain," Walters said. He was tall, sinewy, and wore the official uniform of juvenile delinquents everywhere—leather jacket, jeans, engineering boots. He put his Elvis sneer on right after he brushed his teeth in the morning.

"Right. I wondered if we could maybe talk a little."

" 'We'?" he said.

"Yeah. The three of us."

"About what?"

I looked around. I didn't want eavesdroppers.

"About Linda Palmer."

"My one night off a week and I have to put up with this crap," he said.

"She was a bitch," Gwen Dawes said.

"Hey, c'mon, she's dead," Walters said.

"Yeah, and that's just what she deserved, too."

"You wouldn't happened to have killed her, would you, Gwen?" I said.

"That's why he's here, Paul. He thinks we did it."

"Right now," I said, "I'd be more inclined to say *you* did it."

"He works for Whitney," Walters said. "I forgot that. He's some kind of investigator."

She said, "He's trying to prove that Rick didn't kill her. That's why he's here."

"You two can account for yourselves between the hours of ten and midnight the night of the murder?"

Gwen eased her arm around his waist. "I sure can. He was at my place."

I looked right at her. "He just said this was his only night off. Where do you work, Paul?"

Now that I'd caught them in a lie, he'd lost some of his poise.

"Over at the tire factory."

"You were there the night of the murder?"

"I was—sick."

I watched his face.

"Were you with Gwen?"

"No—I was just riding around."

"And maybe stopped over at Linda's the way you sometimes did?"

He looked at Gwen then back at me.

"No, I—I was just riding around." He was as bad a liar as Gwen was.

"And I was home," Gwen said, "in case you're interested."

"Nobody with you?"

She gave Walters another squeeze.

"The only person I want with me is Paul."

She took his hand, held it tight. She was protecting him the way Mr. Styles had just protected Mrs. Styles. And as I watched her now, it gave me an idea about how I could smoke out the real killer. I wouldn't go directly for the killer—I'd go for the protector.

"Excuse us," Gwen said, and pushed past me, tugging Paul along in her wake.

I spent the next few minutes looking for Pamela. I finally found her sitting over in the empty bleachers that are used for speed-skating fans every Sunday when the ice is hard enough for competition.

"You okay?"

She looked up at me with those eyes and I nearly went over backwards. She has that effect on me, much as I sometimes wish she didn't.

"You know something, McCain?" she said.

"What?"

"There's a good chance that Stew is never going to change his mind and fall in love with me."

"And there's a good chance that *you're* never going to change *your* mind and fall in love with *me*."

"Oh, McCain," she said, and stood up, the whole lithe, elegant length of her. She slipped her arm in mine again and said, "Let's not talk anymore, all right? Let's just skate."

And skate we did.

5

When I got home that night, I called Judge Whitney and told her everything I'd learned, from my meeting with Bobbi Thomas to meeting the two couples at the ice rink tonight.

As usual, she made me go over everything to the point that it got irritating. I pictured her on the other end of the phone, sitting there in her dressing gown and shooting rubber bands at an imaginary me across from her.

"Get some rest, McCain," she said. "You sound like you need it."

It was true. I was tired and I probably sounded tired. I tried watching TV. *Mike Hammer* was on at 10:30. I buy all the Mickey Spillane books as soon as they come out. I think Darren McGavin does a great job with Hammer. But tonight the show couldn't quite hold my interest.

I kept thinking about my plan—

What if I actually went through with it?

If the judge found out, she'd probably say it was corny,

like something out of a Miss Marple movie. (The only mysteries the judge likes are by Rex Stout and Margery Allingham.)

But so what if it was corny—if it turned up the actual culprit?

I spent the next two hours sitting at my desk in my underwear typing up notes.

Some of them were too cute, some of them were too long, some of them didn't make a hell of a lot of sense.

Finally, I settled on:

If only you really love you-know-who, then you'll meet me in Linda Palmer's apt. tonight at 9:00 o'clock.

A Friend

Then I addressed two envelopes, one to David Styles and one to Gwen Dawes, for delivery tomorrow.

I figured that they each suspected their mates of committing the murder, and therefore whoever showed up tomorrow night had to answer some hard questions.

It was going to feel good, to actually beat Judge Whitney to the solution of a murder. I mean, I don't have that big an ego, I really don't, but I'd worked on ten cases for her now, and she'd solved each one.

6

I dropped off the notes in the proper mailboxes before going to work, then I spent the remainder of the day calling clients to remind them that they, ahem, owed me money. They had a lot of wonderful excuses for not paying me. Several of them could have great careers as science fiction novelists if they'd only give it half a chance.

I called Pamela three times, pretending I wanted to speak to Judge Whitney.

"She wrapped up court early this morning," Pamela told me on the second call. "Since then, she's been barricaded in her chambers. She sent me out the first time for lunch—a ham-and-cheese on rye with very hot mustard—and the second time for rubber bands. She ran out."

"Why doesn't she just pick them up off the floor?"

"She doesn't like to reuse them."

"Ah."

"Says it's not the same."

After work, I stopped by the A&W for a burger, fries, and root-beer float. Another well-balanced Cody McCain meal.

Dusk was purple and lingering and chill, clear pure Midwestern stars suddenly filling the sky.

Before breaking the seal and the lock on Linda Palmer's door, I went over and said hello to Bobbi Thomas.

She came to the door with the kitten in her arms. She wore a white sweater that I found it difficult to keep my eyes off of, and a pair of dark slacks.

"Oh, hi, Cody."

"Hi."

She raised one of the kitten's paws and waggled it at me. "She says 'hi' too."

"Hi, honey." I nodded to the door behind me. "Can I trust you?"

"Sure, Cody. What's up?"

"I'm going to break into Linda's apartment."

"You're kidding."

"You'll probably hear some noises—people in the hallway and stuff—but please don't call the police. All right?"

For the first time, she looked uncertain. "Couldn't we get in trouble?"

"I suppose."

"And aren't you an officer of the court or whatever you call it?"

"Yeah," I said guiltily.

"Then maybe you shouldn't—"

"I want to catch the killer, Bobbi, and this is the only way I'll do it."

"Well—" she started to say.

Her phone rang behind her. "I guess I'd better get that, Cody."

"Just don't call the police."

She looked at me a long moment. "Okay, Cody. I just hope we don't get into any trouble."

She took herself, her kitten, and her wonderful sweater back inside her apartment.

7

I kind of felt like Alan Ladd.

I saw a great crime movie once where he was sitting in the shadowy apartment of the woman who'd betrayed him. You know how a scene like that works. There's this lonely wailing sax music and Alan is smoking one butt after another (no wonder he was so short, probably stunted his growth smoking back when he was in junior high or something), and you could just feel how terrible and empty and sad he felt.

Here I was sitting in an armchair, smoking one Pall Mall after another, and if I wasn't feeling quite terrible and empty, I was at least feeling sort of sorry for myself. It was way past time that I show the judge that I could figure out one of these cases for myself.

When the knock came, it startled me, and for the first time I felt self-conscious about what I was doing.

I'd tricked four people into coming here without having any proof that any of them had had anything to do with Linda Palmer's murder at all. What would happen when I opened the door and actually faced them?

I was about to find out.

Leaving the lights off, I walked over to the door, eased it open, and stared into the faces of David and Millie Styles. They both wore black—black turtlenecks; a black peacoat for him; a black suede car coat for her; and black slacks for both of them—and they both looked extremely unhappy.

"Come in and sit down," I said.

They exchanged disgusted looks and followed me into the apartment.

"Take a seat," I said.

"I just want to find out why you sent us that ridiculous note," David Styles said.

"If it's so ridiculous, why did you come here?" I said.

As he looked at his wife again, I heard a knock on the back door. I walked through the shadowy apartment—somehow, I felt that lights-out would be more conducive to the killer blubbering a confession—and peeked out through the curtains near the stove: Gwen and Paul, neither of them looking happy.

I unlocked the door and let them in.

Before I could say anything, Gwen glared at me. "I'll swear under oath that Paul was with me the whole time the night she was murdered."

Suspects in Order of Likelihood
1. Millie
2. Gwen
3. David
4. Paul

That was before Gwen had offered herself as an alibi. Now Paul went to number one, with her right behind.

I followed them into the living room, where the Styleses were still standing.

I went over to the fireplace and leaned on the mantel and said, "One of us in this room is a murderer."

Millie Styles snorted. "This is just like a Charlie Chan movie."

"I'm serious," I said.

"So am I," she said.

"Each of you had a good reason to kill Linda Palmer," I said.

"I didn't," David Styles said.

"Neither did I," said Paul.

I moved away from the mantel, starting to walk around the room, but never taking my eyes off them.

"You could save all of us a lot of time and trouble by just confessing," I said.

"Which one of us are you talking to?" Gwen said. "I can't see your eyes in the dark."

"I'm talking to the real killer," I said.

"Maybe you killed her," David Styles said, "and you're trying to frame one of us."

This was pretty much how it went for the next fifteen minutes, me getting closer and closer to the real killer, making him or her really sweat it out, while I continued to pace and throw out accusations.

I guess the thing that spoiled it was the blood-red splash of light in the front window, Cliff Sykes, Jr.'s, personal patrol car pulling up to the curb, and then Cliff Sykes, Jr., racing out of his car, gun drawn.

I heard him on the porch, I heard him in the hall, I heard him at the door across the hall.

Moments after the door opened, Bobbi Thomas wailed, "All right! I killed her! I killed her! I caught her sleeping with my boyfriend!"

I opened the door and looked out into the hall.

Judge Whitney stood next to Cliff Sykes, Jr., and said, "There's your killer, Sykes. Now you get down to that jail and let my nephew go!"

And with that, she turned and stalked out of the apartment house.

Then I noticed the Christmas kitten in Bobbi Thomas's arms. "What's gonna happen to the kitty if I go to prison?" she sobbed.

"Probably put her to sleep," the ever-sensitive Cliff Sykes, Jr., said.

At which point, Bobbi Thomas became semi-hysterical.

"I'll take her, Bobbi," I said, and reached over and picked up the kitten.

"Thanks," Bobbi said over her shoulder as Sykes led her out to his car.

Each of the people in Linda Palmer's apartment took a turn at glowering at me as they walked into the hall and out the front door.

"See you, Miss Marple," said David Styles.

"So long, Sherlock," smirked Gwen Dawes.

Her boyfriend said something that I can't repeat here.

And Millie Styles said, "Charlie Chan does it a lot better, McCain."

★ ★ ★ ★ ★

When Sophie (I'm an informal kind of guy, and Sophia is a very formal kind of name) and I got back to my little apartment over a store that Jesse James had actually shot up one time, we both got a surprise.

A Christmas tree stood in the corner resplendent with green and yellow and red lights, and long shining strands of silver icing, and a sweet little angel right at the very tip-top of the tree.

And next to the tree stood the beautiful and elegant Pamela Forrest, gorgeous in a red sweater and jeans. Now, in the Shell Scott novels I read, Pamela would be completely naked and beckoning to me with a curling, seductive finger.

But I was happy to see her just as she was.

"Judge Whitney was afraid you'd be kind of down about not solving the case, so she asked me to buy you a tree and set it up for you."

"Yeah," I said. "I didn't even have Bobbi on my list of suspects. How'd she figure it out anyway?"

Pamela immediately lifted Sophie from my arms and started doing Eskimo noses with her. "Well, first of all, she called the cleaners and asked if any of the rugs that Bobbi had had cleaned had had red stains on it—blood, in other words, meaning that she'd probably killed Linda in her apartment and then dragged her back across to Linda's apartment. The blood came from Sophia's paws most likely, when she walked on the white throw rug." She paused long enough to do some more Eskimo nosing. "Then second, Bobbi told you that she'd stayed home and watched *Gunsmoke*. But *Gunsmoke* had been preempted for a Christmas special and wasn't on that night. And third—" By now she was rocking Sophie in the cradle of her arm.

"Third, she found out that the boyfriend that Bobbi had only mentioned briefly to you had fallen under Linda's spell. Bobbi came home and actually found them in bed together—he hadn't even been gentleman enough to take it across the hall to Linda's apartment." Then: "Gosh, McCain, this is one of the cutest little kittens I've ever seen."

"Makes me wish I was a kitten," I said. "Or Sherlock Holmes. She sure figured it out, didn't she?"

Pamela carried Sophie over to me and said, "I think your daddy needs a kiss, young lady."

And I have to admit, it was pretty nice at that moment, Pamela Forrest in my apartment for the very first time, and Sophie's sweet little sandpaper tongue giving me a lot of sweet little kitty kisses.

The Cat's Mother

Mat Coward

"Oh," I said, and then didn't really know what to say next.

It was the first time I'd spoken to my neighbour—he'd moved into the house opposite only recently. In fact, it was the first time I'd even seen him up close. I already had the feeling that the small, bearded man at Number 16 and I were not going to be pals. There was something about his permanent-looking scowl, and the way he had only opened his front door the few inches strictly necessary for minimal communication, that suggested he wasn't the popping-round-for-a-neighbourly-beer type.

"Well," I said, "sorry to trouble you. If it's not your cat—"

"It's not my cat," he said again, and shut the door.

For a moment I considered crouching down and shouting through his letterbox. *"My name's Bill, by the way. Nice to meet you, too!"* But the skinny, all-black cat in my arms was wriggling, and I thought I'd better get him home before he escaped.

I earned a few scratches for my efforts—the inevitable price of trying to be helpful to cats, in my experience—but managed to get us both behind the door to my flat without losing him.

"Well, Lodger," I told him (because you've got to call cats something, even when they're only temporary residents), "this is a little puzzling."

157

★ ★ ★ ★ ★

I'd first spotted him a few days earlier. Watching cricket on TV, I'd been distracted by what I at first took to be the sound of a set of bagpipes being dissected by a one-eyed butcher. I turned the volume down on the telly, got up and peered out at the street from behind my net curtains. The source of the racket was immediately apparent: a black cat, sitting outside Number 16, yelling its lungs out.

The cat didn't seem to be in any real distress; I guessed that its owner was simply late home from work—cats, I've noted, tend to react with outrage to any minor disturbance to their routines. It was too hot to close the window against the noise, so instead I turned the cricket commentary up a couple of notches, and sat back to watch New Zealand getting skittled out by India.

But the next day, the cat was there again—and again the next day. On the fourth day, perhaps because he'd seen me watching him from my window, he gave up on Number 16 and strolled over to my place. I let him in, and he made straight for the kitchen. A saucer of milk shut him up for a while, but only a while; I could tell from his ribs that he hadn't eaten much lately, so I went to the Bangladeshi shop round the corner and bought a couple of tins of moggy nosh.

I let him sleep on my bed for an hour or so (my granny was a midwife, who always maintained that good digestion depended on having "a nice lie-down" after a heavy meal, and I assumed that held good for dislocated cats as well as for pregnant humans), and then, while he was still drowsy, I scooped him up and carried him over to Number 16.

With the discouraging results already chronicled above.

"So who *are* you then, Lodger? If you don't belong with Mr. Friendly, where do you belong?"

By way of reply, Lodger strutted into the kitchen, stood on his hind legs and leant against the fridge, crying loudly. This wasn't difficult to translate from Cat into English. Lodger was saying: "Right now, I belong where the food is. After that, I belong where the bed is. Enough philosophy— let's eat."

The only neighbour I knew at all well was the woman downstairs, named Sri. We'd met over a burst water pipe the previous winter, and it was immediately obvious that we had more in common with each other than either of us did with the rest of the street. Apart from anything, we were both in our late twenties—though Sri, to my mind, dressed more like a seventeen-year-old. All nose rings and black lace from charity shops. Tiny black skirts worn over black leggings. Black eye make-up and dyed black hair.

We saw a fair bit of each other, although—recently single again after a three year live-in—I wasn't looking for anything more complicated. That evening, I went down and knocked on Sri's door. She was wearing her usual smile when she opened it, but as soon as she saw what I held in my arms, she backed off, covering her mouth with a lacy sleeve.

"Bill, don't bring that in here! I'm allergic!"

I started to say sorry, but then she evidently got a closer look at Lodger, because suddenly she was all smiles again. "Oh, it's a *black* cat!"

"It is," I agreed.

"Oh, well, I'm not allergic to *black* cats." Sri laughed, as if the very idea of anyone being allergic to *black* cats was comical. "Come on in, Bill and Blackie."

"Blackie? You know this cat?"

"No," she said, leading us through to the kitchen and

putting the kettle on. "I was just guessing. So the cat isn't yours?" Lodger tried to rub himself against her ankles, but Sri sidestepped him and he almost fell over.

I explained about the cricket, and the bagpipes, and Mr. Friendly. Sri agreed that it was odd. "But why would anyone deny owning their own cat?"

"I don't know. I suppose it's possible the guy got a cat, then decided he didn't want it any more and just kicked it out. You hear about things like that."

"That would be so cruel," said Sri, giving Lodger a sympathetic, if distant, smile. Lodger didn't notice; he was asleep on my lap. Sri made no move to stroke him, I noticed, so perhaps she wasn't as confident as she'd claimed about the exclusion clause to her allergy.

"You don't know the bloke at Number 16, do you?"

"No," said Sri. "Never met him. Why do you ask?"

Her tone was a little sharp, though I couldn't image what I might have said to produce such a reaction. "Well, no reason. Just asking. I mean, as far as you know, he doesn't own a cat? You haven't seen a cat over there?"

"You obviously think I spend all day monitoring the lifestyles of my neighbours, Bill. Well, guess what? I have better things to do with my time."

"Sorry," I said. "I didn't mean anything like that." I still wasn't sure what I'd said that was so offensive—any more than I was sure what Sri *did* do with her time. Somehow, the obvious question, "What do you do for a living?" had never arisen between us. In my case, the answer would have been simple. I'd been in business with my ex-girlfriend, and since the break-up had been what my mother liked to call "between careers." As for Sri—well, with her appearance, I'd worked out that she probably wasn't a bank clerk. Maybe she was a roadie for a punk revival band? Maybe she was between bands.

"That's OK, silly, I'm only teasing," she said, and to prove it she stuck her tongue out at me. I wished she wouldn't do that; it made me feel nauseous. Her tongue had three little earrings through it.

"Anyway," I said, "the long and the short of it is, you don't know anything about Mr. Friendly, you don't know who this cat belongs to, and you—"

"And I'm a fat lot of help," she said, her good temper now thoroughly recovered. "Sorry, Bill. But at least I make good coffee."

Actually, I don't much like coffee. I prefer tea. But Sri wasn't to know that.

I don't know if it's true what cynics say about cats— that they don't care who they live with, as long as there's room service—but I do know that within a short time Lodger behaved as if he couldn't remember ever having been anywhere else. He still hid under the bed every time the doorbell rang, though. Good luck to him—the space below my bed was too low to be efficiently cleaned by my occasional dash-rounds with the vacuum cleaner, and I'd be damned if I was going to start lugging furniture around just to disturb a colony of dust monsters. Sri had said, more than once, that I was "a typical bachelor" in this respect. She seemed to think this was some sort of insult.

One evening, three days after Lodger had moved in, he was driven to seek refuge in the Land of Dust by a long, *long* ring at the door.

Mr. Friendly—the man who claimed not to own a cat— stood on my threshold, panting. He'd obviously just run up the stairs. I didn't know why, but wondered if it had anything to do with the blood that was pouring freely from his nose.

"Hello," he said. "Look, sorry, but I wonder if you can help me."

"In what way?" Perhaps he'd run out of handkerchiefs.

"The thing is, I think I've just killed your neighbour."

"What?" I said. "Which neighbour?"

"It was an accident. She attacked me, I tried to fend her off, and she fell and bashed her—"

"Do you mean Sri?"

"If that's what she's calling herself." He wiped at the blood on his face, smearing it around nicely. His eyes were wild and his movements spastic. "She attacked me, this isn't murder."

"Why would she attack you?" Then what he'd said a few sayings back sank in a little deeper. "Never mind that—where is she?"

She was in the small hallway of her flat, lying on the floor. Her feet were in the kitchen doorway, and her head was propped against the skirting board, halfway to the bedroom. A scalp wound was bleeding impressively.

"She's dead," said Mr. Friendly.

"Looks like it." I knelt down by her and listened for things. I couldn't remember what it was you were supposed to listen for. It involved a mirror, I thought, although I couldn't imagine how a mirror might help you hear better. I took Sri's wrist between my fingers, but I couldn't feel a beat. That didn't mean anything; I once went on a Health & Safety day at work, and I couldn't even find my *own* pulse. It's like dowsing for water: some people can do it, and some people—

"Aaaagh!"

Sri had meowed. I'd screamed, dropped her wrist, and

leapt backwards. In doing so, I'd tripped over Mr. Friendly and banged my bum on the floor.

"It's her cat," said Mr. Friendly. Which reminded me.

"What is your name, by the way?"

"Lew."

"Right. I'm Bill."

"Yes," said Lew. "It wasn't *her* that meowed. It was— well, you know, it was a cat."

I looked round. Lodger must have followed us down the stairs.

"When you screamed," said Lew, "he ran into the bed-room."

"Right," I said. "That wasn't actually a scream, that was merely *aaaagh!*"

This time we both screamed.

"She sneezed," said Lew. "She's not dead!"

"No," I said, "but she *is* allergic to black cats."

We took her to the hospital in my car. I'd suggested calling an ambulance, but Lew insisted that driving her our-selves would be quicker. I couldn't see how my old banger would be quicker than an ambulance, but I did grasp that not arguing would be quicker than arguing, and by then Sri was more or less on her feet, so we got her out to the car be-tween us. She was groggy, and kept one hand against the back of her head all the time, as if to prevent it falling off. She didn't say much, except for once or twice muttering "Go away, Blackie."

Lew sat in the back with her. As my elderly engine coughed into life, I looked at him in the mirror. "She at-tacked you . . . ?"

He sighed. His nose had stopped bleeding. He rubbed it with his knuckles and it started again. He leant forward to speak in my ear. "You know her as Sri? Yeah, well, she's got lots of names. She used to be a private detective."

"A *what?*"

"Specialized in investigating industrial injury claims. She investigated me."

"What was wrong with you?"

"Thanks to her evidence, my claim was disallowed. Unfairly disallowed, I might add."

"What was your injury? What did you do for a living?"

"This is a couple of years ago, right? So now I'm broke, unemployable, living on nothing. Then I hear that your friend Sri has retired from work on—get this—a disability pension. Actually, not a pension: full salary."

"Why? What's wrong with her?"

"Work-related stress-induced agoraphobia." He *could* hear me, then; I'd begun to think the engine noise was drowning my questions out. "She's faking it, obviously. Who better? Who knows the game better than her? So I hired a PI myself—"

"What did you use for money?"

"—tracked her down, took the flat opposite—"

"Hello? Can you hear me?"

"My plan, obviously, was to get evidence against her and turn her in. Same as she did to me."

"And how did this end up making your nose bleed?"

He was quiet for a moment, then he said: "She attacked me."

At the hospital, he helped me get her out of the car, and said, "I'm off."

"Wait a minute! If there's been a—"

"What's your name? Bill? My advice is, keep your nose out. She won't thank you if you don't. Just tell them she fell off a chair changing a light bulb."

"A light bulb?" I said. But he'd gone, and I was left wondering why Lew hadn't called an ambulance instead of coming to fetch me. Or called the police. Or just buggered off.

I told them she'd fallen off a chair changing a light bulb. "A light bulb?" said the nurse.

She was basically fine, they said, but because she'd been briefly unconscious she'd have to stay in for a day or two while they counted her brain cells. Or something.

Once she was settled in bed, I asked her what had happened. "What did Mr. Friendly say?"

"You mean Lew?"

"Right."

I told her Lew's story.

"Well . . ." She stared at the ceiling for a time. "I am in hiding from him. Hence the Gothy look."

"You're in disguise?"

"And I am on long-term sick leave."

"From being a private eye?"

"But I didn't attack him. He attacked me."

"Why would he do that?"

Sri closed her eyes and ran a palm over her brow. "I don't want to talk any more, Bill. I feel weak."

"All right. Do you want me to report this to the police?"

"No!"

"Only, if someone attacked me in my own home, I'd definitely—"

"No harm done, Bill. He's gone. What's the point in getting a load of hassle?"

She was getting drowsy. As I got up to leave, I said: "Blackie sends his love."

I could just make out her mumble: "Bloody animal. . . ."

* * * * *

First thing I realised when I got home was that I'd locked Lodger inside Sri's flat. I fetched the spare key from my place, and found the cat sleeping on Sri's bedspread with his chin pointing towards the ceiling. I carried him upstairs. He slept through the journey.

Back at Sri's, I stripped her bedding and put it in the washing machine, which already contained a small pile of laundry. I spent about forty minutes trying to figure out how to work the bloody thing, and as soon as I got it going it started making a horrible clunking noise.

I couldn't figure out how to switch it off mid-cycle, so I just sat there in Sri's kitchen, chewing my lip down to the gristle, until the wash was finished. The clothes seemed clean enough. So did the gun. The gun was squeaky clean. It was wrapped up in a pale pink t-shirt and it smelt of soap powder.

I'd never seen a real gun before. Strange thing: they're actually *bigger* in life than they look on TV. Which is how you can tell them apart from the actors who wield them.

I remade Sri's bed with the clean bedspread, had a glass of water (in lieu of a glass of brandy), then I wrapped the gun up in the pink t-shirt and put it back in the machine. I thought of checking to see if it was loaded, but I didn't know how to do that without setting it off.

Back in my own flat, I fed Lodger—not before time, in his opinion—and wondered who he belonged to.

Had to be either Mr. Friendly Lew, I figured, or Sri Many Names. Or perhaps both jointly, if the private eye story was crap and they were an ex-couple. She'd left him, probably because he was violent, he'd come after her, and . . . what? The cat followed him? He brought the cat with him for purposes of moral blackmail? "See how *thin* poor little Blackie is? He hasn't eaten since the day you left home."

Maybe I'd got it wrong; the cat was just a stray who'd happened to pick Number 16 at random. Or because sixteen was his lucky Lotto number. Or because he could smell that the house didn't already have a cat in residence.

Sri wasn't in a talkative mood when I visited her the next morning. It was left to me to make conversation. Such as:

"By the way, I washed your bedspread. The cat had been on it."

"You washed it?"

"I was worried, you know, about your allergy."

"Right. Thanks. That's great. Was there—was the machine working OK?"

"The machine?"

"It's been playing up."

"No. Yeah, no, it was fine."

When I got back home, on my way up the stairs, I could hear someone moving about in Sri's flat.

Oh, *good,* I thought: more excitement.

"How did you get in?"

"I used a skeleton key," said Lew, pointing at a sledgehammer propped against the wall.

"You'd better get out. I'm calling the police."

He shrugged. "She wouldn't want you to do that."

"Why not?"

"Because of the cat." He smiled a cat-like smile. I had no idea what he was talking about. Or smiling about. Was he threatening Lodger?

"Listen, Lew, the cat is—well, never mind where the cat is. The cat's safe. You can't use the cat against her."

He was still smiling. "It doesn't matter where the cat is."

I shook my head. Not like a cat, more like a confused person. "Did you find what you were looking for?"

Lew took a step towards me. It wasn't a big hallway, otherwise I'd have taken a step back. "What do you know about it?"

"Nothing," I said. "But you're obviously looking for something."

He nodded, looked at me, picked up his sledgehammer. "I'm going now. My advice? If you're still thinking of calling the police, speak to Sri first."

"Because of the cat?"

"See? You're getting it."

I closed the now lockless door behind him, put the security chain on, then checked the washing machine. The gun had gone.

"We were investigators," said Sri, later that afternoon, after I'd told her straight, no argument, that as far as I was concerned a stolen gun was cop stuff. A stolen *illegal* gun.

"You worked for the same firm?"

"We *were* the firm, Lew and me. Partners. We investigated compensation claims—the story he told you was based on truth, because he didn't know how much you already knew."

"He needn't have worried."

"Don't sulk, Bill. Scientists believe it contributes to penile shrinkage." She closed her eyes. "We used to make a little extra cash—and I don't want you to comment on this, OK, because you weren't there—by approaching certain of the targets—"

"The fraudulent ones."

"Shut up, Bill. And offering to put in a favourable report

to their employer or insurance company, in exchange for a slice of the compo."

"How you missed becoming a nun, I'll never understand."

"Then Lew came up with the idea of expanding the con—threatening to put in *unfavorable* reports on *genuine* claimants."

I thought about that, my scowl meeting my sneer halfway. "That idea is almost as stupid as it is evil."

Sri turned up her hands. "*Crazy* idea. One scam too many. Lasted about ten minutes before we were shopped."

"Were you nicked?"

She tried to blush, but she'd lost a lot of blood. "He was. I . . ."

" 'Wasn't'? Is that the word you're looking for?"

"I had a friend in CID."

"You got off?"

"No, no. My friend warned me the cops were coming, and I . . ."

Her pauses were beginning to get on my nerves. "You decamped the scene."

Sri smiled. "I decamped. Lew served twelve months. Ever since he got out, he's been looking for me."

"He feels you betrayed him, I suppose. On account of you *did*."

"I suppose he must. Anyway, he found me, obviously. Took that flat opposite. I spotted him, and I decided I needed protection."

"You went for the illegal firearm option over, say, the rape alarm."

"Well, Bill, be fair—prison can drive people mad. I really think it drove Lew mad. He was behaving mad."

I said: "Whose cat is Blackie?"

"So I put a note through his door saying, let's talk things through. I thought I'd threaten him with the gun, and he'd—"

"Was it loaded?"

She frowned. "I bloody *hope* so. I assume ammunition was included in the price. When you buy a car, they put petrol in it, don't they?"

"Why didn't he decamp, when he thought he'd killed you? You showed him the gun, he chose to thump you instead of running away, he thought you were dead—why did he come and fetch me?"

"Terror," said Sri. "Did he look scared? I bet he did. He's a scammer, Bill, not a killer. I was unconscious, and I'll bet he was thinking, 'If she dies, it won't take the cops long to associate her with me.' He needed damage limitation. Get his story on record first—she asked me over here, then she attacked me, I defended myself, she slipped. It's unlikely he'd be charged with anything, in the absence of any evidence to the contrary. He'd be questioned for a week and a half, sure, but not charged."

"He hid the gun in the washing machine."

"I thought that was where it'd end up. A man of unimaginative habit, poor old Lew. Used to keep the off-the-books money in his washing machine. I suppose he thought the story would be less complicated if he kept the gun out of it. Not so much for the cops to get tumescent about."

"So whose cat is it?"

"By the time we arrived at hospital, he'd obviously decided I was going to live after all. So off he went."

"But not for long."

She yawned and said, "I think those pills are beginning to take effect. I'm beginning to feel rather—"

"What will Lew do with the gun?"

"Don't worry, he'll dump it. He doesn't want it, he just wants me disarmed. He'll probably sell it to a toddler."

So, I thought: *if he wasn't interested in the gun* . . .

"He was looking for the money, wasn't he?"

She closed her eyes. "Money?"

"The off-the-books money from the washing machine. From the scams you two were running."

"Well, *yes*, I suppose he *might* have been, now that you come to mention it."

"Before you went on the run, you had time to grab the ill-gottens, but no time to warn your partner."

She blew me a kiss. "I suppose you could put it that way, yes."

"That's why he's been watching you, not confronting you. Trying to figure out where it was. He knew it was unlikely to be in a high-interest account or a pension fund, seeing as you're wanted by the police."

"True," she said. "You can give a false name to a hospital, but a bank needs documents."

"Bloody bureaucrats."

"Quite."

"Do you think he found it?" I said. "The money."

She smiled, and replied with confidence. "No."

Next morning, they told me she'd checked out. Against advice.

She wasn't at home. I was pretty sure she hadn't *been* home, either, because I'd been keeping an eye out. Not for her—for him. There was no reply from Lew's place, Number 16. Maybe she'd killed him. She didn't seem the kind to kill in cold blood, just for money, but until yesterday she hadn't seemed the kind to blackmail fraudulent industrial injury claimants. Whatever kind that was. And

171

why had she invited Lew over the other night, if not to
bump him off?

There wasn't much in her flat; it was minimalist, like her
personal colour scheme. I found no sign of any banknotes
or bearer bonds or gold bullion. I did find a mobile phone,
under her bed. Amongst the numbers listed—very few, including me and the pizza delivery—was one for 'Mum'.

A woman answered: "Isobel Inch."

"Hello—is Sri there, please?"

Sri's mum hung up. I looked up "Isobel Inch" in the
London phone book.

It took me an hour and a half to drive to Mrs. Inch's address, and when I got there I was obviously too late. For
what, I had no idea, but there were police everywhere, and
an ambulance standing by. An ambulanceman was standing
by the ambulance, smoking a roll-up.

I took a pen in my hand and clicked the top. "Hi," I
said, "can you give me anything? The press office isn't answering the phone." I didn't have a notebook to go with my
pen, but I hoped he wouldn't notice.

He didn't. Or he didn't care. "Some mad bird's stabbed
some bloke."

Sri. She'd gone to her mother's, Lew had followed, but
this time Sri had chosen a weapon she could handle.
"Christ, lovely. Is he bad?"

"Quite bad, yeah," said the ambulanceman. "He's
dead. After she stabbed him, she called the cops, they
called us. My partner's in there now. When we got here,
she was going on about how this dead bloke had stolen her
cat."

Seven police officers emerged from the house. In their
midst was the accused man-stabber. It was a middle-aged
woman.

* * * * *

The CID came round the next day. I told them that yes, a young woman I knew as Sri did live here, and that I knew her "to speak to." Yes, I'd taken her to hospital the other night; she'd slipped off a stool while changing a light bulb. Yes, Sergeant: a *light bulb*. No, I hadn't seen her since she discharged herself from hospital—had no idea where she was. Convalescing somewhere, maybe? Anyway, what's all this about—is she in trouble?

"Her mother is. She killed a man yesterday. Self-defence, she says—this man had killed her cat, allegedly, and then come back for her. Or so she reckoned."

It was her *mum's* cat. Lodger. Blackie. So when Sri saw the cat in my arms, she knew it could only be a message from Lew: I've visited your mother, I've stolen her cat, who knows what might happen next if you don't come through with the money? Sri didn't get the gun to defend herself from Lew—or to avoid sharing the washing machine money. She got the gun to kill him with, because she was right—he *had* gone mad—and she couldn't see any other way of protecting her mother.

Lew left the cat outside all day, expecting Sri to see it. But he didn't realize—she was too busy watching *him* to notice poor old Blackie.

The detectives were waiting for me to comment on this fascinating example of human behaviour. "Reckons he killed her cat?" I said. "Why would he do that?"

The cops shrugged. "Who knows? Drugs, probably."

They'd figure it out in time, once they checked Lew's record against known associates. Meanwhile, I wasn't going to help them. Apart from anything, I wasn't sure how many laws I'd broken in the last few days. Failure to report an assault, failure to report an illegal firearm . . .

unlawfully harboring a fugitive cat.

Poor Mrs. Inch. Had Sri told her *anything* about what was going on? Did she really think Blackie was dead? I had no way of knowing until—or unless—Sri got in touch with me. For now, I could maybe risk an anonymous letter to Mrs. Inch at the remand prison: "Don't worry. Blackie safe and well. Will be waiting for you when you get out. Save up your prison pay, I will be invoicing you for cat food, pet litter, and flea drops."

Sri did get in touch. A postcard of a London bobby, smiling. You can buy them just about anywhere in Britain— or abroad, for all I know. The postmark was illegible on the card's shiny surface. The message was brief:

"Sorry about ev/thing. Your real friend. Please look after B. Kiss-kiss, S. "

And that was it. Except for the PS: *"You shd clean under yr bed more often!"*

I puzzled over that for a minute or two, then I went and had a look under my bed. Then I went to ask Blackie the Lodger which he would prefer for his lunch: steak or caviar?

In the Lowlands

Gary A. Braunbeck

"Do you know how a hobo feels?
Life is a series of dirty deals
Except for a kind word, a cup of coffee
And the song of the wheels. . . ."
—Anonymous message scrawled on boxcar wall,
Kansas City, 1934

There's an old superstition among hoboes—especially those whose camps are made near the switch yards—that a 'Bo's death is mourned by the whistles of two passing trains; the sounds meet overhead in the night and, though each might be a bit mournful when heard by itself, they combine to create a pleasant song of welcome for the 'Bo's soul as he takes himself that last, great freight to Heaven.

When you hear that sound, you're supposed to remove your hat (if you wear one), close your eyes, and wish that fellow's soul good travel to the Pearly Gates, then say a little prayer that the body he left behind finds its way to the Lowlands—that is, that some good soul will see fit to give it a proper burial and not just leave it where the fellow shuffled off the ole mortal coil.

A second blast of the dual train whistles serves as a message to let you know that his soul found its way home and his remains have been properly sent to the Lowlands. That's about the best a 'Bo can hope for when he leaves this world.

175

Fry Pan Jack told me about that legend right before the TB finally overpowered his body and he passed on, leaving his cat, Billy, in my care. I heard the trains cry for him that night. And I put his remains in the Lowlands myself, reading a passage from Jack's Bible after I finished tamping down the soil.

Now I've got to stand trial for my life before a jury of my peers.

All of this in the same week.

It happened like this:

It was as good a jungle as a 'Bo could hope for in that spring of 1933: On the sunny side of the hills, within walking distance of a fairly clean creek, and not too far from a couple of switch yards and coal bunkers; a thick patch of trees offered shelter from the chilly night winds, and the town dump was within spitting distance and ready for scavenging; add to that the friendly atmosphere that greeted a fellow upon his arrival—and sometimes just getting past the railroad bulls was cause for major celebration on the parts of all residents—and, well, you'd be crazy to think you could do better.

Billy and I had decked a rattler—that is to say, rode spread-eagle atop a passenger train—for about the last half-hour before we jumped. (*I* did the actual jumping; Billy just sort of curled himself up into a ball inside my pack and hung on for dear life.) My landing was nothing to write home about—in fact, I thought I might've twisted my ankle (not the case, I'm pleased to tell you)—but luckily we were far enough away from any yards or stations that I didn't have to worry about any bulls seeing me.

Not that I've got anything against railroad police, understand. Most of them are fairly good sorts but there's always a couple wherever you go who make sport of cracking open

a 'Bo's skull. Seems those types can't tell the difference between a bum and a hobo—and believe you me, there's a difference. As Jack used to say: "Bums loaf and sit; Tramps
loaf and walk; but a 'Bo moves and works and he's clean."

Even on the road there's a hierarchy—and I learned myself that word from a dictionary Jack gave to me. "Nothin'll
catch folks off-guard quicker than a 'Bo with a good vocab-
ulary, son; shows 'em you got brains and folks're more
likely to give a decent meal to a man with some brains
who's willing to work than a moron."

Add to that formula a hungry pet—like a cute cat—and
you're hardly ever turned away.

I suppose that's one of the reasons Billy and me found
ourselves so welcome at this particular jungle that evening.

There were a couple of fellows standing watch over a pot
of Mulligan stew in the center of the camp; they were the
first to spot me. They'd been talking up 'til then, but once
they got sight of me their conversing stopped and they just
stared at me.

One by one, the other men in the camp took notice of
their silence and had to have themselves a look at what was
going on.

Every man there was staring at me as I walked toward
the fire and the pot.

"Evenin'," I said, tipping my hat.

"Where you coming from, stranger?" asked one of the
Mulligan Stew Boys.

"Michigan way. Found a couple days' work helping to
unload coal at the River Rouge auto plant."

"Was they still needin' workers when you left?"

"That they were."

He considered this for a moment.

I knew what was going through their minds: *Is he on the*

level or is he a damned yegg?

A yegg was any one of a number of disreputable fellows who posed as a 'Bo but didn't want to be bothered with actually *earning* his keep, and so made his way by robbing an honest traveling laborer. A yegg wouldn't think twice about beating up or even killing a 'Bo for whatever the man had on him.

I set down my pack and untied it—not enough that Billy could stick his head out and attract even more attention—but enough so that I could reach inside and remove a potato and an onion, which I offered to the Mulligan Brothers. They were more than happy to take it.

You never, ever walk into a 'Bo camp and not offer something to go with the evening's meal if you can help it. That's part of the code. Not that they'd let you go hungry—if there's a meal being cooked up in a camp, then that meal is for everyone there and anyone who might happen by. Just because there's a code, that in no way means that fellow 'Bo's would let a man starve.

The camp warmed up to me fairly quickly after that, and when I later pulled out some recent newspapers and detective magazines that I'd managed to pick up along the way, well, you'd have thought I was one of the Permanents there. The three things you can have in your pack which will always make you welcome in any camp are coffee (or tobacco), food, and something for the fellows to read. Life on the road is lonely—that's a given—but it can also be boring as hell and a recent newspaper or a story magazine can offer a man something to occupy his mind with besides the worry of where his next job and meal might be coming from.

It was only when we were sitting down to dinner that Billy woke up and started raising a ruckus inside my pack. I reached in and pulled him out and from the way the rest of the camp reacted, you'd have thought I'd produced a wad of greenbacks.

"Well, damn my eyes," said the bigger of the two Mulligan Brothers—who went by the name of Cracker-Barrel Pete (you never use your real name in a camp and never ask a man for his)—"Why didn't you tell us you had yourself a little fur-ball with you?"

"He was sleeping when I got here and he doesn't take kindly to being woke up from his beauty rest." The fellows laughed at this.

"You know, don't you," said Pete, "that there's a couple restaurants in town that'd be happy to give a day-old fish to a cat like your, uh—he got a name, your cat?"

"Billy."

Pete nodded. "Yessir. Never fails to amaze me, human nature, that is: Folks who wouldn't give you a slice of moldy bread would hand over something small and fresh for a hungry cat."

I knew that to be true enough; many was the time when Jack and I almost met with the business end of a proprietor's shotgun until they caught sight of Billy; then we almost always left with a tin of sardines or tuna. A can of tuna, mixed with some crushed cracker, sometimes lasted the three of us a couple of days.

Pete's words did not go unheard by the others.

"Say," he said, leaning over and refilling my coffee tin, "think you and Billy there might be up for a little excursion in the morning? Might find yourself a day's decent work, plus old Billy there might snag us some special goodies for tomorrow's dinner."

"Don't see why not," I said, letting Billy get comfortable in my lap. I picked a small square of potato from my stew and fed it to him. Billy liked potatoes—onions, too, which often made his breath a holy terror. "Folks seem to take a quick shine to him."

"Then it's settled," Pete said just loud enough that the others would know I was more than willing to do my share. "First thing tomorrow, we'll go into town with Billy and hit the bakery there, see if we can't get ourselves some day-old bread or pastries—he like pastries, does he?"

"Billy's a pastry fool."

Pete laughed. "Ain't that something? A cat that likes pastry!"

We all had ourselves a good laugh then at Billy's expense, but he didn't seem to mind; an animal of sweeter nature you'd be hard-pressed to find.

I couldn't help noticing, though, that the other Mulligan Brother—a thin reed of a fellow calling himself Icehouse Willie—wasn't laughing like the rest of us; oh, sure, he was chuckling away so's to fit in, but I caught something in his eyes as he looked at Billy that didn't sit right with me.

Maybe I'm just tired, I thought, and would not allow myself to think unkindly of anyone in the camp that night.

I read a few news articles to some of the men who couldn't read themselves, then we passed another hour or so passing around one of the detective magazines, taking turns reading serial chapters (and a juicy one this yarn was, too!), then, long about ten, with the stars above us in abundance, we found our spots for the night and got as comfortable as the ground would allow.

Just before I dozed off, Billy's terrible breath on my cheek on account he'd decided to sleep on my arm, I heard a train whistle in the distance, echoing low and lonely, and I closed my eyes, wishing Jack a good night, as well.

As if to echo my sentiments in his own unique way, Billy

sneezed in my ear, yawned, then dug in his claws and conked out.

Long about three in the morning (I checked the position of the stars, something Jack had taught me to do, in order to guess about the time) I woke up and pulled Billy off my arm, sitting him down next to me. He gave a grumpy, sleepy-faced look—*You'd better have a damned good reason for this*—then sat back on his hind legs and stared.

"Shh," I whispered so as not to awaken anyone nearby. "Just . . . just stay right there."

I reached into the bottom of my pack (which I'd been using as my pillow) and pulled out a small piece of smoked salmon wrapped in tinfoil—a little treat I'd bought for Billy with some of my Michigan wages at a Japanese place in Cedar Hill, Ohio the day before. I would've offered it to put in with the stew, but Billy had been a little out of sorts lately—Jack having only left us a week ago—and I figured the fellow would enjoy a little late-night treat.

That's when I heard the cry.

It wasn't so much a *scream*—it had been strangled in the throat before it could get to that point—but there was enough panic and underlying misery in the sound to let me know that whoever had made it was either being killed or in the middle of a right terrible dream.

I did a quick look-round the camp and saw Pete a few yards away with the other Mulligan Brother, Icehouse Willie—the one who'd been looking at me and Billy so strangely. Pete had Willie's head pressed against his chest and was covering Willie's mouth with one of his hands. Willie was crying fiercely, deep, body-wracking sobs, his eyes closed tight, his face getting redder and redder, and as I gently put Billy down and started over to see if there was anything I could do to help, I saw that Pete was rocking his

181

buddy back and forth like he would a baby, and all the time whispering, "It's okay, Willie, there you go, there you go, no fires, okay? It's a nice, cool night and you're out here in the open with me and you're okay, shhh, there you go, it's okay. . . ."

It took a few more minutes of this before the other man finally fell back to sleep.

I hoped for his sake that it was a peaceful slumber.

Another quick look-round showed me that the man's cries had awakened a few of the residents, but they acted as if they were used to it and so simply rolled over and went back to sleep.

Pete came over to me, shaking his head. "Sorry about that. Guess we should've told you about Willie."

He gestured toward the far end of the camp and we set off walking. When we were almost to the edge of the camp he stopped for a moment, a sad look crossing briefly over his face. "I don't mean to sound cold-hearted, but Willie, he's . . . he's not quite right in the head, understand? Lost his wife, Carol, and his little girl, Sandy, to a boxcar fire about a year ago when they were riding to Chicago. I was riding that same train, only I was in a different car. Terrible thing. He tried to get to them, but they were in a hay-car on account the train was hauling a lot of cattle, and the flames . . . well, you get the idea."

". . . yeah . . ." I whispered.

"Sometimes he talks about 'em like they were still alive." He reached up and squeezed the bridge of his nose. "Damnedest thing, though. The folks who were ridin' in that car . . . well, shit, you just *know* better than to light any kind of match in a hay-car. I mean, light's a bad idea in the first place on account it can tip off the bulls, but in a *hay-car!*" He shook his head. "We had just pulled out from a stopover when the fire broke out, understand? And most of the people in that car had been asleep. Willie and his family, they were sitting way in the back of the car so's they'd face everyone . . ."

"Best way to protect a family, under the circumstances."

"That may well be, but I heard later from a couple of the folks who got out that a bull set that fire—just came running up alongside and tossed in a match. Someone hadn't closed the door all the way." He shrugged. "It happens. Them cars, they can get damned stuffy." He looked back to where Willie was sleeping quietly, then looked at me and lowered his voice. "Just between you and me, though, I always thought Willie must've gotten a look at the bull who done it, and maybe part of what makes him . . . not quite right anymore is that there just ain't enough room in him for both his grief and his wanting to get revenge on the sumbitch what set that fire."

By now we'd started walking back into camp. I looked at Pete and grinned. "It's really decent of you . . . I mean, taking him on like you have."

Pete grinned back. "That obvious, is it?" A shrug. "What the hell else was a God-fearing man supposed to do? Couldn't very well leave him to his own devices, not in the shape he's in. Yeggs'd make a meal of him and not even leave bones for the dogs. And lately—hell, ever since we came to this camp three, four weeks ago—he's been gettin' a lot worse. Not just the dreams, those're bad as ever, but he's . . . he's acting less and less . . . uh . . ."

". . . rational?"

"—yeah, that's the word. He's been actin' less rational when he's awake. Scares me, y'know? Man's been a good traveling companion and I think of him as a friend, but if he gets to the point where I can't handle him no more. . . ."

183

He let the words and thought trail off. He knew I didn't need to hear him complete that sentence.

"How'd he come to be called 'Icehouse' Willie?"

Pete told me, and his answer damn near broke my heart.

I stopped by my sleeping spot where Billy was still sitting impatiently, waiting for his late-night treat.

"Cute little bugger, ain't he?" said Pete.

"Not so loud. He's full enough of himself as it is."

Pete smiled, reached down and petted Billy's head, then gave me a tip of his hat and went back to his spot beside Icehouse Willie.

I laid back down and got as comfortable as I could, then peeled away the foil wrapping from Billy's treat and placed the chunk of salmon in front of him. "There you go, pal, enjoy yourself."

Billy sniffed at it, decided it was to his liking (why he always made of show of *deciding* he wanted to eat something I could never figure out), then dug in, savoring every bite.

I had to admit it looked sort of tasty and made my mouth water slightly—and it wasn't as if I'd never shared Billy's meals before—but I figured he deserved this special treat all to himself.

I stroked the fur on top of his head. "You're a good traveling companion, Billy."

He sniffed once in mid-chew as if to say, *Yeah, yeah, yeah, I'm a prince and so're you. Now can I please get back to the business at hand?*

I laughed under my breath, then rolled over and fell back asleep.

The last thing I remember thinking was how I hoped that Willie could sleep the rest of the night without hearing the cries of his wife and daughter.

Damnedest thing, really, the trouble that little secret snack of Billy's caused later.

Jack was an old-timer on the road (he admitted to being ". . . in spitting distance of seventy, but I ain't gonna tell you in what direction"), and many was the night he'd regale me with tales of his adventures on the road before I hooked up with him.

One of his favorite memories was of a house in Portage, Wisconsin he'd spent time at a few years back.

"The mother there, her husband had died a year or so before, and what with a family to care for, she had to find a way to make herself a respectable living. She took in washing, cooked meals for others, and baked up something like forty or fifty pies a night for a little restaurant called the Pig-n-Whistle. All that pie-cooking, it took a powerful lot of stove wood.

"Now, her children couldn't keep up—poor woman had to have at least five long rows of stacked wood that needed to be split—so she was more than happy to offer a 'Bo a job splitting the logs. You could earn yourself a fine, fine meal splitting wood for her. The jungle we lived in was just a few hundred yards from her back yard, on the other side of the rail yard in a grove of trees by Mud Lake. 'Bo's tended to hang around that jungle for a good long while, not just because of the work and meals this lady'd provide us with, but because if it was your birthday and her kids got wind of it, she'd bake up a little cake and send it over, and her kids . . . well, they always managed to come up with sort of present for you, a magazine or book or old toy. Yessir, it was a good place. Many's the night, after the wood had been split and the pies baked and the evening meal served, she'd invite any 'Bo who wanted to come over and sit on her porch and listen to the radio. She always served something to drink on those nights. I remember her lemonade best, on summer evenings with the radio playing and the trains whistles calling in the distance.

"Yessir, that's my idea of Heaven. In fact, that's where I first found old Billy here. He was one of a litter of kittens that someone tossed in the river one night, all tied up in a bag. If me and this other fellah—can't recall his name now—but if we hadn't been where we was and seen this happen, all them kittens would've drowned. Terrible thing, the way people treat their pets."

"What about they way they treat each other?"

He looked at me and shook his head, grinning. "You expect too much of others, son. Take my advice—if you expect no kindness, then you won't be disappointed when none is given; but, Lord, are you all the more grateful for it when it *is!*"

I was awakened from my pleasant dream of Jack and the Pie Lady when someone slammed a steel-toed boot into my hip. I came awake with a shout, grabbing my pack and spinning around on the ground, ready to swing at whoever'd done that to me, when I found myself staring up at one of the most unpleasant-looking bulls I'd ever seen. He stood there, big as life and three times as ugly, holding his club in his hands and looking all-too-ready to open up my skull.

And if he wasn't up to messing up his uniform with my brains, one look at the younger fellow with him told me *he* was ready.

A little too ready, from the glint in his eyes.

The big bull stared down at me. "Understand you came in here around six, six-thirty last night, that right?"

"Yessir," I said, looking around for Pete and the others. They were gathered together near the cooking area, trying not to be too obvious about looking at me.

I looked around quickly myself, wondering where Billy had wandered off to.

"Look, officer," I said, "I don't want any trouble. If you'd be so good as to tell me what this is all about—"

He snapped the business end of his club forward and thrust it into my chest. I took this as a request to shut up and listen.

"There's been rumors about a yegg moving through these parts," the bull said to me. "Don't get me wrong, boy—I got nothing against the likes of 'Bo's, but last night—early this morning, actually, around four-thirty, five—someone from this camp broke into a couple of stores and stole themselves a bunch of food, liquor, and a little bit of money."

He squatted down to get his face close to mine, still keeping the club in my chest. "Reason I know they were from this camp is because it wasn't enough for them to be happy with the stores. No—they had to go and break into some folks' *homes*." He made a quick sideways gesture with his head. "Pete over there told me you're the only new fellah what's come around here lately. Sorry to say, but that makes you—"

"—your best suspect, yessir."

He studied me for a moment. "The only reason I don't have the sheriff out here with me is because, one, I didn't think you'd be stupid enough to come back here and, two, I think it would sit better with the folks who were robbed if I could go back and tell them that the 'Bo's took care of the problem in their own manner . . . if you read my meaning."

And I did, all too clearly.

You live in a camp, you don't rob from another hobo. You live in a camp, thievery of any kind was to be avoided outside the camp as well—or at least kept to a minimum; a pie lifted from its cooling spot in an open bakery window every now and then, some vegetables hurriedly snatched from a garden, or an old shirt clipped from an outside line, that was acceptable if the circumstances warranted thieving, but if it could be avoided, you did so. Townspeople were your only source of jobs and handouts, and you did not— repeat, *did not*—do anything to anger them. One dirty yegg could muck it up for everyone in the camp, and a good camp near a good town—especially one where the bulls didn't run you off on a regular basis, as this seemed to be— well, that was to be respected in the same way people respect the church they go into every Sunday.

The bull looked at his partner and said, "Watch him while I search his pack, Carl."

Carl's idea of watching me was planting one of his feet right into my chest and pressing down. Hard.

"*Carl,*" said the other bull. "What'd I tell you about that?"

"Bastard broke into my *house*, McGregor."

"I know that your place was one that he hit, but until we find something of yours or one of the other folks—" He stopped, then looked down as he pulled a half-empty bottle of whiskey from my pack. He followed that with some bread, cheese, and a couple emptied cans of salmon.

None of which had been in my pack the night before.

"Looks like we got our man, Carl." Then McGregor pulled out an envelope with some writing on it. He read it, looked at me, then his partner, and handed the envelope to Carl.

"What's this?" asked his partner.

"You tell me. It's got your name on it."

Carl glared at me—now I was sure there was a craziness barely hiding behind his eyes—and snatched the envelope from McGregor, tore it open, and removed the letter inside.

He tried to control it, that I could see, but whatever was written on that page rattled him something fierce.

"Well?" said McGregor.

"Huh? Oh—it's, uh . . . it's just a letter I got from, uh . . . my granddad." He folded the paper up in a hurry and stuffed it into his pocket. "You piece of—" he said to me, pulling back his foot to kick me.

"Carl!" snapped McGregor. "This ain't that Illinois rat-trap you moved here from. We don't strike a man without bein' provoked."

"I can't help it! It's bad enough to break into a man's house and steal his food and whiskey, but what the hell kind of yegg steals a man's personal *mail?*"

"The kind we just caught."

McGregor stood up and gestured that I should do the same. As soon as I was on my feet Carl spun me around and slapped handcuffs on me—none too gently, I might add—then marched me into the center of the camp and sat me down on an old tree stump.

"One way or another," Carl snarled in my ear just low enough so only I could hear him. "One way or another you're going to the Lowlands."

My mouth went instantly dry. The violence in his voice was like nothing I'd ever heard before, and there was no doubt in my mind that Carl wanted to kill me with his own bare hands . . . and whatever was in that letter was the reason.

"Okay, fellahs," said McGregor loudly enough to get the camp's attention. "My shift ends at five. I got three other

189

guys from the yard who're willing to sit on the jury. I'll stand in as bailiff. You got until then to pick out the other nine jurors."

Pete stepped up and said, "You be the one who calls Judge Carson?"

"I'll take care of it—and I'll make damned sure the people in town know that you fellahs are gonna take care of this problem. I'll offer apologies, if it's all the same."

Pete nodded. "And if it's all the same to you, McGregor, I'll be defending our friend here."

"Ain't no friend of mine." He turned to me real quick and said, "Nothing personal. If you're innocent, I'll apologize to you. Until then, you're as good as a crook in my eyes." He grabbed up a small coil of rope someone had scavenged from the dump and ordered a couple of men nearby to tie my legs and ankles to the stump.

"Be seeing y'all this evening," he said, tapping the end of his club against the brim of his hat.

Carl walked by me real slow.

Real slow.

Not blinking.

One way or another . . .

Everyone in camp watched the two bulls make their way over the hill and back toward the rail yard. Then Pete put a hand on my shoulder and said, "You know what the penalty is for that kind of thieving, don't you?"

I nodded my head.

If found guilty, they were bound by the code to either kill me or exile me.

You exile a 'Bo by marking his face; that way, he'll not find himself welcomed in any camp he comes across thereafter.

I have seen such marked men in my travels. Burned

faces, faces missing an eye, an ear, a nose . . . a simple scar would be treasured as a symbol of mercy. But mercy was something you rarely found under these circumstances. Not only was a marked 'Bo not welcomed in a camp, damn few people will give him work or a handout.

Death or marked exile; wasn't much of a choice, when you got right down to it.

The rules of the road can be brutal when a bad element threatens to ruin it for the innocent.

I looked up at Pete. "You seen Billy?"

"No, I ain't. And that's how come McGregor went right for you."

"Beg pardon?"

"Whoever broke into them places had a cat with him. A couple of witnesses saw it. Guess the guy stole a fish or two from one of the markets to feed it."

"Oh, brother . . . there were a couple of empty cans of salmon in my pack."

"Not yours, I take it?"

"No."

"Now let me ask you something."

"Anything."

"Am I the only one who's noticed that Willie is conspicuously absent this morning?"

I looked at his face and knew there was no need for me to answer.

The trial got under way a little after four p.m.

It didn't help my chances much that Eastbound Earl, the prosecutor, dumped the contents of my pack onto the ground to reveal the evidence that McGregor and Carl had found there.

It also didn't help much that Billy finally put in an appearance a few minutes before the trial started, his breath stinking of fish. He bounded right up to me and jumped into my lap, rubbing himself against my coat.

"I have to say in all fairness," whispered Pete, "that this does not bode well for your, uh . . . your—"

"—acquittal?"

"I was going to say something a little more colorful— mentioning a particular point on your anatomy—but 'acquittal' will do. Look, we both know full well that Willie's the one who snatched Billy up and took him into town when he did all that stealing. I *told* you he ain't been actin' like himself since we got here. Probably figured things would go just like they have up to this point. Hell, wouldn't surprise me one bit if he actually made an effort to be seen."

"He knew that any witness would remember the cat more than his face?"

Pete nodded. "If there was even enough light for them to see his face."

". . . yeah . . ." I whispered.

"Don't get me wrong, he's the one who did this, but the rules don't allow for his, uh, condition to be taken into account. Thief's a thief, and that's all there is to it."

We both searched the crowd of faces until we found Willie, standing way in the back of the spectators and looking for all the world like a man who was walking in his sleep.

"We'll hear the defense's arguments now," said Judge Carson, a hard-looking older gentleman whose voice sounded like he gargled with moonshine three times a day. Pete told me that Carson had ridden the rails once himself and had been treated well by the hoboes he encountered, and so always oversaw these trials. "He's as fair as you're going to find."

"Pete," said McGregor, our bailiff.

Carl stood off to the side, trying for all the world to look like he didn't want to slit my throat.

"If it please the court," said Pete, standing just a bit taller than usual, "I would like to call Mr. Icehouse Willie to the stand."

There was a murmur among the spectators, and when Willie didn't come forward right away, McGregor—our inspiring bailiff—said, "All right, Willie, let's—"

—and that's when Pete pulled me to my feet and led me up to the witness chair.

McGregor stopped and stared but said nothing.

He knew damned well—as did every other resident of the camp—that I was not Willie, but no one said a thing.

"What the hell're you doing?" I whispered.

"You remember our talk last night?"

"Yeah . . . ?"

"Just try and follow my lead. And remember that Willie stammers."

I glanced in Willie's direction; he gave me a nervous, almost apologetic look as Pete started in on his questioning.

"Okay, Willie, why don't you tell us why you—"

"Thief!" someone shouted.

The camp crowd reacted with appropriate shock.

Judge Carson banged his gavel, calling for order.

"Would you please tell us," said Pete, "why it is you're called 'Icehouse' Willie?"

I was never much for play-acting, but I gave it my best try; can't rightly say why, but I *trusted* Pete. "Ah, hell, Pete . . . what's that got to do with—?"

"Answer the question, please," said Judge Carson.

"Pete here, he g-gave me that name."

Judge Carson stared at me, then at Pete. "I'm gonna assume here that this has some kind of bearing on the case?"

"It does, Yeronner; it might not seem, ah . . . uh . . ."

"Evident," I whispered from the side of my mouth.

"—evident right away," said Pete, "but it will come to bear on things."

Carson sighed and nodded his head. "Just don't go off on any tangents, understand? My daughter's bringing my new granddaughter over for supper tonight and I'll be damned if I'm gonna miss seeing them."

"Understood, Yeronner." Pete turned his attention back to me—but not before making a quick gesture with his head and eyes that told me I should look over at Carl.

I did so, and saw a 'Bo offering the bull a bottle of beer. Carl accepted—not gratefully, big surprise—and had a little trouble getting the top off. While he struggled with the bottle opener, the 'Bo who'd given him the beer brushed back behind him—

—and slipped something from his pocket.

I looked at Pete to let him know I'd seen it. I'd told him about the letter earlier that day. Evidently he'd taken it upon himself to obtain the thing without Carl's cooperation—Carl being so warm-hearted toward hoboes as he was. It probably would have seemed like taking advantage of the man's good nature to ask him for it.

I went on, remembering as best I could what Pete had told me of Willie's story last night. ". . . and after the fire, the bulls put all the bodies in this here icehouse near the yard. I . . . I, uh . . . I w-w-went in there to find my Carol and Sandy and after I f-found 'em I wanted to sit with 'em awhile, y'know? Sandy, she don't like to be left alone when she's sleeping, and Carol, sh-she'd give me h-h-holy h-hell if I went off while they was resting. . . ." I made up this last part, which might have been stupid, but by that time I found I was enjoying playing this part; so much so that I felt a tear slip down my cheek—wasn't hard to muster tears at the thought of how terrible Carol's and Sandy's last moments had been—then I simply sat there, staring at the ground and shaking.

"Go on," said Pete, softly.

". . . you come in there after a bit and made me leave before I f-froze to death." Then I remembered something Pete had told me Willie once said: "Sometimes I wish I had. Least then we'd all still be together."

Judge Carson slammed his gavel against the wood tabletop that served as his bench. Someone had scavenged the table from the dump earlier; it smelled of old and rancid food and decay and probably accounted for the pained expression the Judge's face had been sporting since this got under way.

"All right, Pete, that's enough," said the Judge. "Whether or not this has any bearing on your case, I don't care. It's damned depressing and I, for one, will not sit here and be made to listen to a man re-live something as terrible as losing his family."

"May I ask one more question, Yeronner?"

"Best make it a good one."

I saw Pete glance over in Carl's direction; that glance was not lost on McGregor, who, for the rest of the proceeding, kept looking from Carl to Pete to me to Willie, then back again.

"Willie, did you see the man who set that fire in your boxcar that night?"

Carl froze, blanching.

I shot a quick glance in Willie's direction; he looked straight at me with one of the most lonely, scared, and pained expressions I've ever seen deform a man's face, then

195

gave a short, sharp nod of his head.

"I'm a bit deef these days," snapped Judge Carson. "You're gonna have to actually *say* something."

"Oh, yeah," I said. "I saw him real good."

Carl looked about ready to dump in his shorts.

I had just a moment before figured out what was in that letter and who had written it.

What I didn't understand was the why of the rest of it.

"*O-kay,*" said Judge Carson, slamming his gavel once again, "that is more than sufficient for my tastes. We are here to try this man"—he snapped a liver-spotted hand in my direction—"for thievery and breaking and entering. I must be gettin' soft in the head, lettin' you pull a stunt like this—"

"But, Yeronner—"

"But *nothin'*, Pete." He looked directly at me. "Are you guilty of the crimes of which you're being accused?"

"N-nosir."

Carson smiled. "All-righty, then." He glared at Pete. "Now, we have heard the prosecution's arguments and seen their evidence, I have the statements of the townsfolk whose business and residences were broken into, so now it's your turn. That's how this works, Pete, it's called a *trial*. They go, then you go, I listen to all pertinent statements. Dull, I know, but I *like* dull. So . . . do you have any witnesses to call who might actually have something to say about the case that I'm *supposed* to be hearing, or should we just go right to the closing statements?"

Pete looked at me, then Carl, then Willie.

"One moment, please, Yeronner," Pete said.

"What the—?" I whispered to him when he came over to me.

"You a gambling man?"

"I don't—"

"Shh, hang on."

The 'Bo who'd picked Carl's pocket came up to Pete and handed him the letter. Pete made a fairly big show of accepting the letter, opening it, reading it, then considering what he'd just read.

"Yeronner," he said, "I have no other witnesses to call, but I would ask a favor of the court."

"Oh, *hoo-ray*," muttered Carson. "What is it?"

"A twenty-four-hour recess."

Carson mumbled curses under his breath, then said, "If I ask you why, is the answer going to upset me?"

"Probably."

"I should've retired last year like Mildred wanted." A sigh, then: "All right, why do you want a recess?"

"Some new evidence has just come to light which might prove my client's innocence."

Carson was silent for several moments, then said: "You're kidding?"

"Afraid not, Yeronner."

"The man was discovered with several of the stolen items on his person—not only that, but several of the stolen items were either fresh or canned fish—and *don't* think I didn't get a whiff of his cat's breath earlier. Between its breath and the smell on its fur, it could knock a buzzard off a shit-wagon."

"It looks bad, I know."

"This is such a help," I said under my breath.

"We're talking not only about the thieving here, Yeronner, but a man's life, as well. I'm willing to personally vouch for my client. Twenty-four hours."

Carson looked at his pocket watch. "No . . . but I'll give you some time. It's just right now six. Even though it's gonna have Mildred spittin' nails at me, we will reconvene

197

at this same spot at nine a.m. tomorrow morning. Is that sufficient time for you to gather and examine your new evidence?"

Pete's smile was almost evil. "That'll be more than enough time, Yeronner."

I looked back to where Carl had been standing.

He was long gone.

One way or another. . . .

And Pete—with more than a little help from Willie—had just turned me into bait.

"Nine a.m.," repeated Carson. "But after that, new evidence or no, some sort of action has to be taken, understand? If someone isn't punished, the town's gonna want me to have McGregor and his friends bust up this camp and send all of you on your way. I'd hate to see that happen. I know a lot of you fellahs—if not by name, then by sight—and find you a decent sort for the most part.

"Until nine a.m., then"—he cracked his gavel against the table top—"this court stands in recess."

Pete looked at me and winked.

"*Please* tell me you know what you're doing."

"I sure hope so."

I looked down at Billy, whose expression seemed to say, *Me? I wanted to keep going, but you just had to stop and make some new friends, didn't you? If Jack was here he'd hit you on the head so hard you'd have to unzip your pants to blow your nose.*

"Next time, I'll listen," I whispered to him.

Then Billy yawned. Easy to do when there's no chance your body'll be in the lowlands come this time tomorrow.

It was close to midnight and I was freezing.

Billy lay curled up in my lap, fast asleep.

I had been moved outside the camp, to a special "holding area" that McGregor and one of the jury bulls had set up—according to Judge Carson's instructions—before all the Law Boys left for the night.

I was still in handcuffs, though my legs had been untied so I could at least stand from time to time and stretch. McGregor and the jury bull had taken a group of 'Bo's down to the dump and hauled back a couple of discarded railroad ties which they proceed to set upright into a portion of soggy ground. The mud pulled the ties down about two feet before the things hit solid rock and stayed in place. Then one of the cuffs was opened and my arms were stretched behind my back and cuffed again behind the two ties—both of which extended to a good three feet past the top of my head. I didn't have a lot of room for moving, but at least it wasn't so tight that I couldn't relax my shoulders a little.

But only a very little.

Pete and Willie had made themselves pretty scarce after I was secured, and for the better part of the last four hours it'd just been me and Billy, sitting in the cold night air with little more than cricket-song and starlight for company.

Trees still surrounded me—in places pretty thick.

A man could hide himself pretty well in those trees.

I had a feeling I knew what was going to happen, and why it was that no one in the camp—McGregor included—had spoken up to say that I wasn't Icehouse Willie.

It was all a crap-shoot, and while I don't discourage a fellow from taking himself a big leap of faith every once in a while, it feels a bit different when a possible snake eyes will come attached to a real snake of sorts, one filled with venom and ready to end your life in a heartbeat.

I looked down at Billy's sleeping form and jostled him with my legs.

Nothing.

I tried once more.

Billy made a little mewling sound in the back of his throat, dug his back claws in just a little bit deeper, but still didn't wake up.

"Wish to hell I could sleep like you," I said to him. "You have any idea how that used to burn Jack up when we was on the road together? He used to say that you could probably sleep through a train wreck that was caused by an earthquake that took out an iron bridge." Then I laughed. "There were times he wondered whether or not you were deaf."

"What happened to your stammer, Willie?"

I snapped my head up just in time for my eyes to meet the business end of a .38.

"You should've known better than to try and catch a free ride on any line I worked for, Willie," said Carl, looking crazier than even before. He gave me the once over, then stepped back and gestured with his gun for me to stand up. "I don't like the idea of killing a man who's not on his feet, even though you goddamn tramps barely qualify as men, you ask me."

I thought that last remark should be left unanswered, so I shimmied myself up into a standing position, much to Billy's chagrin; he finally let go of my leg and dropped onto the ground, stretching, yawning, and hissing.

"Cute cat," said Carl.

"I get a lot of compliments on him, thank you."

Carl stepped forward again and pressed the barrel of the gun to the middle of my forehead. I was amazed that I didn't wet myself, I was so scared.

"Tell me one thing," he said.

"Anything to keep the conversation goin' as long as possible."

A smile slithered across his face like a worm. "Good that you can crack wise right now. Be a good idea if you kept a pleasant thought in your head."

In the distance I heard the whistle of a train.

Far off, from the opposite direction, it was answered— though not yet joined—by the cry of another train.

"How'd you see me, Willie? I mean, I was pretty fast on my feet and that door wasn't opened all that far, I just ran up and tossed in the lit book of matches . . . how'd you get a look at me?"

"I d-don't quite r-r-remember." The stammer this time wasn't play-acting on my part; I was scared right down to the ground.

Carl considered this for a moment, then shrugged, pulling back the hammer. "So I didn't get everyone in the boxcar. I guess I can live with that."

Billy had by now wandered over down by Carl's legs and was rubbing himself up against the bull's steel-toed boots.

Carl kicked out a bit but that didn't deter Billy; once he decides he's going to rub up against you, you just resign yourself to it and that's all she wrote.

"Dammit to hell!" Carl snapped looking down and giving Billy a more insistent kick—

—and that's when the gun slipped away from my forehead, a little off to the side—

—and that's when I heard a voice yell, "Duck!" from somewhere in the nearby trees—

—and then there was a blast from somewhere that sparked right above my head and sent Carl to the ground cussing and flailing and blew away a good foot of railroad tie above—

—and before I knew what was happening, I felt someone toying with the handcuffs.

"Don't make a sound," said Pete, who was in front of me.

"Who's messing with the cuffs—?"

"Willie," Pete replied. "Did I forget to mention that he used to be a locksmith?"

I twisted my neck so as to look beside me. "That true?"

"B-bad locks in t-t-town," said Willie, working the cuffs open with some sort of pin. "Bad and ch-ch-cheap, easy to break in, easy, easy, easy."

The cuffs came off and I took my pack when Pete offered it.

Carl still lay on the ground a few feet away, cradling his right hand against his chest. There wasn't any blood but his hand looked to have been burned pretty good. The cylinder of his .38 gleamed in the moonlight pooling near my feet. I looked around and saw the rest of his gun a few feet beyond that.

McGregor came walking up to Carl, holding a mean-looking pump-action shotgun in front of him.

"Helluva shot, ain't he?" said Pete.

"A true marksman," I replied, shaking so much I thought I was going to drop.

Trailing behind McGregor—and looking for all the world like the most cantankerous so-and-so you'd ever want to meet—was Judge Carson. Two sheriff's deputies flanked him.

I looked at Pete. *"And . . . ?"*

"Okay, okay, sorry. Look, me and Willie, we been keeping close to Carl ever since Chicago. We figured it was only a matter of time before he wound up transferred to some little 'burg like this and we'd have time to . . . well, see if we couldn't do something about what he done. The trick was being able to stay in one place long enough to get the trust of the camp."

As he spoke, I noticed the other residents of the jungle, awakened by the gunfire and yelling, were shuffling toward us from down below.

"They had a helluva time convincing me," said McGregor over his shoulder. "I know Pete and Willie here fairly well, and I knew when Pete pulled a stunt like he did earlier today—you know, calling you up to testify like you were Willie . . . I figured something pretty serious must be going on."

I nodded. "That's why you didn't say anything?"

"That's why no one who knows the two of them didn't say anything. 'Course, that letter of Willie's that Carl had on him was a pretty convincing piece of evidence. That, and what he just now tried to do to you."

Carl was still, evidently fascinated by the barrel of McGregor's pump-gun.

"I'm real sorry that we did this to you," said Pete, putting a hand on my shoulder. "But we had to distract ole Carl's attention there in order to have time to convince McGregor and the Judge that Carl here's the fellah that set that fire in Chicago."

"Twelve people died in that fire," said Judge Carson. "Be they hoboes or not, it was murder. Some parts of this country still look poorly upon that."

"Judge," I said, nodding my head.

"That was quite a performance you gave this afternoon," he said. "Mildred's going to get herself quite a laugh out of it when I tell her."

"How was dinner?" I asked.

Carson shuddered. "Oh, it was great, seein' my daughter and granddaughter, but my wife still can't make a decent gravy." He put a hand to his belly. "I was already up when McGregor came by with Pete and Willie. I figured even if this turned out to be a bust, I'd at least be out in the open when that gravy made me start sounding my horn . . . if you get my meaning."

The Judge and McGregor, along with the two deputies, hauled Carl to his feet and cuffed him with the same cuffs he'd used on me. I'd be lying if I said I didn't get a certain amount of enjoyment out of seeing that.

I looked at Icehouse Willie. "Why'd you have to take Billy?"

"Sandy likes cats, that she d-d-does. Likes 'em a lot. Was always asking me for one. Her mother, though—" He whistled quick and low. "—can't stand the things. M-m-make her sneeze something terrible."

He was crying as he told me this.

"No one's g-g-gonna burn today, nosir, not while I'm around, nosir. No one's gonna burn. The Lowlands aren't g-g-gonna take anybody today, nosir."

Pete slapped my back. "C'mon, we got to get the hell out of here."

I heard the cry of the approaching train whistles.

"Where's Billy?"

Willie opened his coat. "S-snug as a bug."

Billy was nestled comfortably in one of Willie's massive inside pockets.

Judge Carson looked at us, then toward the train whistle. "You know, this here's gonna draw a lot of attention from folks for a while. Me and McGregor and the deputies, we all heard Carl's confession. The rest'll be fairly easy." He came up to Willie. "Justice will now be served, Willie. Your Carol and Sandy, they can rest easy now. So can you."

And with that, they hauled Carl away.

I turned and looked at the rest of the camp; they had stopped several yards away and were now making their way back to their beds, cricket-song and starlight accompanying them.

Life on the road is hard, but sometimes you make new and good friends.

"You in the market for a couple of extra traveling companions?" Pete asked.

"The more the merrier," I said as the four of us took off up the hill and over the rise toward the tracks.

We decked the rattler just outside the switch yard, disembarking a few hours later just a few miles from the Canadian border. From there we caught a lumber car.

We've been a team ever since.

Some nights Willie wakes up from his bad dreams about his wife and daughter. That's when Billy helps the most, soothing his night terrors while I tell him all about Heaven, as Jack saw it. Then we smile at each other, finding peace in the thought of Jack and Sandy and Carol all sitting on that back porch under a summer night sky and sipping lemonade while the radio plays on. A good end to a good day's labors.

And no train whistles mourning.

The Lowlands can't touch us here.

Hell Matter

Jean Rabe

It was barely evening, the sun just set, and the smell of the wet earth was strong. The rain—it had rained all afternoon—was nearing an end, I thought, as the sky was merely spitting now and then in an irregular rhythm that I found most annoying.

I hated rain.

I hated it especially when in this, the height of Missouri's summer, it did nothing to cool things. Somehow despite the time of day, it only served to make everything steamy and more uncomfortable, and thoroughly, thoroughly sodden. Had I not sequestered myself just beyond the opening of this cave I would have been thoroughly wet too, and hot and miserable—rather than dry and only slightly miserable, and terribly, terribly bored.

As I watched the slowing drops, I heard the cicadas start their song. And from somewhere off I heard a steady and repeated slosh and crunch, the heavy sound of men's boots tromping through puddles and across stretches of gravel. An unremitting "shush" told me they were dragging something. Perhaps they would come past this cave and I would have something to watch other than mud and rocks. And if they talked, I would have something to listen to other than this odious drizzle and the simple drone of insects.

I waited, and after several moments the sloshing and shushing grew louder, and the rain began to drum harder— making me realize it had only teased me moments ago into thinking it might stop. The wind picked up suddenly, sending some of the rain inside. There was a flash, lightning. The rumble of thunder followed. I retreated farther into the dry darkness, listening to a patter that was coming angrily now, listening to the sloshing, to the men, who had finally started talking and who were slogging uninvited into my favorite cave. I hoped they were only coming inside to escape the storm, and that they would leave when the rain no longer toyed with me and truly stopped. I did not care to share this place.

"Hate this rain," one said.

I was amused at this, that a man would have something in common with me.

"The weather's nothing to be bothered up about. It's good that it's raining," the other said. I could tell that there were only two of them. "It'll cover our tracks. Folks're staying in their houses tonight. No one saw us leave town. No one way out here to see us."

Except me. I could see fairly well in the growing darkness.

What they'd been dragging was a boy, their hands under his armpits. They dropped him when they came even with me, the shorter man letting out a deep breath, thankful to be free of his burden. The boy didn't move, and I wondered if he was dead. I didn't much care for boys, as I'd met more than a few mean ones in my years—pelting me with rocks, tying things to my tail, chasing me, trying to set my fur on fire. I didn't much care for boys at all. But I didn't want this boy to be dead. I didn't want him rotting inside my favorite cave and fouling the air.

The taller man pulled a small lantern from a pack. He fumbled to light it, as I crept 'round a rock to keep out of sight. From the shadows I continued to watch them, glad that my boredom was banished and still worried that the boy was dead and would soon begin to stink.

I have a keen memory, and so I recognized the men from my trips into town. They were disparate, and it seemed odd that they would keep company. I'd seen the taller one along the river, where the steamboats and barges tie up. He dressed finer on the bank, all ruffles around his neck and wrists, gold rings flashing on each hand, hair smoothed back and dark as oil, and head topped with a cap with a shiny black brim. An important man. But the rings didn't flash much in the lantern's soft light, and he was dressed in the color of night, clothes in good repair, though not so fancy as his river attire.

The shorter one? His clothes were dark, too, but old and spotted. Not an upmarket soul. He had the craggy, drooping face of a bulldog, and he walked with his right foot turned slightly out. I remembered seeing him most often in the shadows of the town's buildings, sometimes in the backs and in the alleys, where people carelessly threw out food. That's what I went into town for, the discarded food. I was getting older and slower, and only old, slow mice were finding their way into my belly. I'd come to—sadly—appreciate the people's garbage.

The boy? I might have seen him, too, but I would not have recalled it—I did my best to avoid boys. In truth I hated them only a little less than the rain.

"We should tie the boy up," the tall one announced. "Don't want him running off on us."

Not dead, I sighed gratefully. There would be no horrible odor in my favorite cave.

"Tie Sammy up? He ain't going anywhere, Hobe. You walloped him good. He's unconscious."

The tall man nudged the boy with his boot. "Mebee he's

unconscious. Mebee he's not. Could be playing possum. We can't take any chances he'll slip away." He fumbled in his pack and pulled out a length of rope. The two men propped the boy up against the opposite wall of the cave and tied his hands behind his back, then tied his ankles together. He was a lean boy, with a hawkish nose and unruly hair. His clothes were worn and thin, holes at the knees and elbows, and he was caked with mud from being dragged here.

"Not sure I like this, Hobe, killing a boy. I ain't got no hankering to. . . ."

"Can't take any chances, I told you. 'Sides, who's really going to miss him?"

"I hear tell he works for Joseph Ament. So Ament'll miss him."

"Ament can find another cub," the one called Hobe said. "I'm not willing to take the chance. I'll not go to jail 'cause some boy heard us jawing."

"Should've drowned him in the river, then," the shorter man said. "Wouldn't've had to come way out here in this weather. Sammy's always down by the river, folks'd think he slipped."

A shake of the tall man's head. "My crew's on my boat. An' there're a few hands working on the river—in spite of this weather. Someone might've seen us. Nobody'd see us around here."

The shorter man shrugged, drawing his shoulders up practically to his ears. "Guess you're right, Hobe. No one comes out to these caves, 'cept some kids, maybe a trapper once in a while."

"That's right."

"And I guess we're not really killing Sammy, eh, Hobe?" He let out a raspy chuckle. "We ain't doing the actual deed. The cave'll do that, eh?"

Hobe didn't reply. He was in his pack again, this time re-trieving something I had no name for. I noticed the boy was stirring behind them and mumbling something.

"Sammysammysammy," the shorter man said, the words hissing together like a teakettle left too long on the stove. "Shouldn't've been out in this weather, Sammy." He started tsking, and he added a finger wag for emphasis. "Shouldn't've been creeping around behind the Hawkins' house. Shouldn't've overheard us."

"Didn't hear nothin'," the boy managed. He poked out his bottom lip. "Didn't hear. . . ."

The tall man roughly backhanded the boy, pitching him onto his side. The boy groaned.

"Sammysammysammy," the other man hissed. "I bet you heard me an' Hobe just fine. I bet you heard real good."

"I didn't hear nothin', I said. But even if I did, I wouldn't tell," the boy offered. "Ain't nobody would be-lieve me anyway."

" 'Cause you're just a kid? Or 'cause you're always telling wild stories? I might go along with you, Sammysammysammy. But Hobe, here? Captain Hobart? He's not the type to take a gamble. Can't afford to." The shorter man bent over and righted the boy. "Hobe says you've got to die." The two men worked quickly then, dou-ble-checking the boy's ropes.

"I didn't hear nothin'. And if I did, I wouldn't tell," the boy repeated. "Honest."

Hobe let out a clipped laugh. "If you're Ament's cub, you'd tell him about me—and mebee, just mebee he'd be-lieve you. Can't have my ship jeopardized 'cause of you. Can't risk losing all I've worked for. Can't go to jail. You understand, boy."

"I could leave town," the boy continued, the desperation thick in his voice. "Go south to St. Louis or east to Springfield. My folks wouldn't miss me. My Pa died last year."

"How old are you, boy?" Hobe leaned close.

"Thirteen."

"You won't be seeing fourteen."

Hobe started backing toward the cave's entrance, and taking the object I couldn't name. He stuffed a cord in the center of the thing and motioned to his fellow.

"Someone's gonna find you out!" the boy hollered to them. "What you're doin' is wrong. Someone else'll overhear you. You can't steal from people like you're doin'. It ain't right." His defiance grew with his hopelessness. "And if I get out of here, Captain Hobart, I aim to see that you and Jim rot in jail forever. You're pirates!"

"Pirates? Told you the boy overheard us," Hobe said.

"Didn't think he knew my name," the short man said, as he returned to the boy and stuffed a rag in his mouth to quiet him. Then he snatched up the lantern. "All shit and no sugar, Sammysammysammy. You're just too dangerous to let live. Light the fuse, Hobe. The way it's thundering, ain't no one going to hear the dynamite."

Then the men were outside, and suddenly the object I couldn't name was sputtering and sitting in the cave's mouth, the cord attached to it burning merrily. I hesitated, looking between the boy and the way out. A part of me was urging me to follow the men, not to stay here. A part of me somehow knew 'here' wasn't safe. But I was curious about the boy. Aren't all of my kind so vexed with a natural inquisitiveness? And so I hesitated and crept closer to the boy. I heard the thunder boom outside, and felt a trembling beneath my paws, heard a hurtful, rumbling clap of thunder coming from the cave mouth—louder than anything—and it

211

set the stone floor to shaking. In an instant my favorite cave was quaking, sending bits of rock and dust down on me like rain. The dust was so thick I found breathing difficult. The rumbling continued, and I was tossed about, the cave trembling like a frightened beast, its walls cracking, the ground continuing to pitch. For the first time ever I felt a true, profound fear, and as my heart hammered loud in my ears, I fully expected to die.

The utter darkness was sudden and absolute. The entrance to the cave was gone, and the rocks that filled the once-opening kept the twilight and lantern light from slipping inside. Kept all hint of light at bay. I sensed my stomach was rising into my throat. The dust continued to come down, and I struggled to take a breath.

I was surprised I didn't die. And as moments passed, the trembling subsided. The only rumbling now came from the thunder I knew was booming outside. The boy was still alive, as I could hear his ragged breath. I couldn't see him, though, couldn't see anything.

I'd found myself in this terrible blackness once before, when I'd ventured so far into this cave the light didn't reach me. I retraced my steps on that occasion. On this occasion, I didn't know what to do.

"Mmmmph." This was coming from the boy.

I didn't like boys. But. . . .

I padded close to him, relying on my hearing and sense of smell. He continued to make the "mmmphing" noise. He smelled of sweat and fear and the wet earth that clung to his threadbare clothes. I could tell that he was struggling against his ropes, and he jostled me in his gyrations as I slid past.

"Mmph?" He'd felt me, and he stiffened and stopped wriggling. If it was possible, his breathing became more rushed and ragged.

I didn't like boys at all, but I moved around behind him, my whiskers brushing first against his fingers, then the rope. I started gnawing, and finally his breathing slowed. When I'd cut through enough of it, he managed to work his hands out. In the blackness he fumbled for the gag in his mouth, then set to untying his ankles.

"Who're you? What're you?" he asked.

Of course, I couldn't answer in a way that he could understand.

Then his fingers were groping through the blackness, finding me and grabbing, fluttering for me when I slipped away.

"A cat," he pronounced. He kept his voice low. "You're a cat."

I felt the air stir, his fingers still futilely searching for me. He gave up, and I heard his feet scrabble over the rocks as he stood.

"Thank ya cat," he continued. "Thank ya mightily."

Faintly, I heard his arm brush against the cave wall.

"My head hurts somethin' fierce," he said. "That ol' Captain Hobart hit me hard."

His feet started shuffling away from me. He grunted, finding the collapsed entrance and trying to move aside the rocks.

"Ain't gonna be able to get out the way I came in, cat. Not that I want to run into them thieves again anyway. They'd surely kill me this time. Shoot me or. . . ."

His feet were shuffling again. Now I could tell he was going deeper into the cave.

"Don't think I been in this cave before," he continued to prattle. "Unless I came in another way."

I'm not sure what I expected of the boy, but it wasn't this—going farther into the utter black. I wanted him to move all the rocks that had fallen down in the entrance. I chewed him loose, and in payment I wanted him to dig us out of the cave.

He continued to move away from the entrance. That he couldn't see didn't seem to worry him overmuch.

"You here, cat?"

I relied on my hearing to follow him, keeping what I guessed was a safe distance. One could never trust boys . . . even ones who owed you.

"I gotta find me a way out, ya know. I can't let ol' Captain Hobart and Junkman Jim get away with it."

I wondered just what it was the two men were getting away with. And though I doubt the boy was able to sense my thoughts, he supplied the information.

"Them two is bad," he continued. "And they's right, I overheard 'em. I was on my way to Laura's house. She was gonna help me with some schoolwork. They was in the alley behind her house, talkin' so fast they sounded like bees. Seems ol' Captain Hobart keeps real close watch on his steamboat passengers. Finds out who's got money and jewelry. And he finds out which gamblers won big stakes."

He paused in his words and steps. I heard him bump against stone. "Careful, cat. Find the wall and press close against it. There's a drop off, and I don't want to find out how deep it goes."

I took his advice, though I was certain I would have felt the edge of any rocky ledge and could have stopped myself from tumbling. We traveled very slowly now, until he was certain the footing was safer. I heard a rustling overhead.

"Bats," he said.

He spoke the obvious.

"They ain't gonna bother us none if'n we don't spook 'em." His course was taking us still deeper, and we were twisting down one unseen path after another. There were other sounds intruding, a plopping of drops on water.

"Maybe I have been in this cave before."

Finally I sensed that we were moving up. The going was more difficult, as the boy was constantly bumping into stalagmites and rocky outcroppings.

"Junkman Jim. . . . When ol' Captain Hobart docks his steamer, I think he goes straightaway to Jim. Tells Jim about the passengers, which ones to follow, which boarding house they're staying at. He tells Jim which ones to rob, and they split the take. They's been doin' it for some time, cat. I'm Ament's cub, all right, and so I read every paper he prints. There's always somethin' there about a robbery. Every week, it seems. Wealthy folks that came down the river and are only stoppin' in Hannibal for a day or two. No one stayin' here long has been robbed. Bet this has been goin' on for better than a year. They's pirates, Hobart and Jim."

The boy continued to chatter as he stumbled, lost. "I gotta get me out of here, cat. I gotta tell Ament, gotta get to the judge so Hobart and Jim can be stopped. Ain't right what they're doin'." He stopped suddenly. "And more than stealin', cat, they's guilty of tryin' to kill me. My head's still achin'. They's gonna be in jail a long time."

We started down again.

I don't know how long we meandered disoriented. Hours upon hours, I was certain. It was long enough that the pads on my feet were sore and bleeding and my legs ached like they'd been set on fire. My throat was dry and my tongue felt thick. I was so very, very thirsty. And hungry. I'd intended to go to town after the rain stopped, to search through the people's garbage.

"You there, cat?" The boy had stopped again, and by the

rustling of his clothes, I could tell he was sitting. "I gotta stop for a piece, catch my breath." His fingers were questing through the darkness, and in an uncharacteristic move, I let him touch my fur. "Yep, cat, you're still there." He settled back against a wall, and I lay nearby. Every few minutes his fingers fluttered along my back. "I like cats," he said.

Perhaps this one boy was all right.

He dozed for a time. I could not sleep. The darkness and my thirst were too disconcerting. Eventually I nudged him, and he clumsily got up.

"Guess you want to get goin', huh, cat? Me, too. Gotta stop ol' Captain Hobart and Jim. They's gonna give the river and steamboats a bad name. I aim to be a steamboat captain someday, cat. An honest one."

I had to nudge him twice more in the hours that followed, on the latter occasion prodding him to his right, where I felt the air moving. My senses were far superior to his, and I knew that if I did not take the lead now, we would either die of starvation in this black place or fall down some hole and break our necks.

The air smelled fresh, and this sped my sore paws. In it I could pick out traces of damp earth and wildflowers. And when I listened closely, and shut out the sounds of the boy's shuffling feet and quick breath, I could hear the cry of some bird and the tinkling of a nearby creek. And I could hear the cicadas singing their blessed, monotonous tune.

I nudged him a final time, and by now I think he heard the sounds of outside, too. He became clumsy in his excitement, slipping on skree and falling to his knees more times than I bothered to count. I fell back so he would not tumble on me, and I only took the lead again at the very end, when a grayness intruded into the black and the insects' song grew louder.

"Hurry, cat," the boy urged, though he didn't have to. I had moved several yards ahead, and my legs were working with a speed they hadn't shown in quite a while. "I've found us a way out of here!"

You found us?

It was only minutes later that we stumbled out of the cave. The air was warmer out here, but for once I didn't complain about the sweltering summer. There were stars overhead, evidence we'd passed an entire day in the cave. I was exhausted, and I stretched out on the ground. In a moment I would worry about the creek and getting a drink. In a long moment.

"We have to hurry, cat." The boy was looking down at me, hands on his knees, and sucking in great gulps of this August air. "We have to get into town and tell Ament about ol' Captain Hobart and Junkman Jim. We gotta get the judge."

I raised my brow. *We?* We didn't have to do anything. We were out of the damnable hole in the ground. We were safe. The creek was near. With some effort I rose and trotted to it and started drinking. The boy was talking again, but I let his words drift to the back of my mind and I concentrated on the sound of the water.

"We gotta go," he said.

You can go where you please, I thought.

Then he scooped me up and nestled me under an arm. I was squirming in protest, but my motions were so feeble, so completely tired was I. I knew the boy was heading into town—Hannibal, he called the place. And so I finally stopped squirming. I was hungry, and Hannibal would feed me. It was night, and so I would be able to pick through people's garbage undisturbed. And then I would find somewhere to sleep.

217

"It's only a mile," he continued. "Not far. Me and Laura used to come out here once in a while. Don't think it was to that cave, though. Ain't never goin' back to that cave."

I agreed with him. I could find a better place to stay out of the rain, and somewhere not so far from town. The past several times my legs had been arguing with me over the journey between town and my once-favorite cave.

Somehow the boy managed to pick up his pace, and as we came down a hill I could see the town's sparse lights. It was late, as most of the homes were dark, but there were streetlights burning. Perhaps this Ament the boy was intent on seeing had left choice scraps outside his backdoor.

It didn't take us long, and we were darting down one street, then down a dark alley. Soon he was bounding up front porch steps and pounding on a door. The boy was impatient, and he began rocking back and forth on his heels, fidgeting with his free hand, then he was pounding again. A light was lit inside, and I could hear slow footfalls and a thin voice.

"Give me a minute." Then the door swung open and a stoop-shouldered man, barechested and in creased pants, loomed over us. "Sam?"

"Mr. Ament," the boy began.

"It's late."

"I know, Mr. Ament, but . . ."

"Samuel, you weren't at work today. I needed you. I have a mind to fire you and get me another cub. One that won't . . ."

"Mr. Ament, Captain Hobart and Junkman Jim just tried to kill me . . . and all because I overheard 'em talkin' behind the Hawkins place." The words flew furiously from the boy's lips. He left nothing out, though the part about our escape from the cave was not nearly as harrowing as he made it seem. The boy was quite the storyteller. When he was finished, Ament shook his head.

"Sam, I usually don't mind your tall tales, but this one is a bit too stretched. If you made it up to justify why you didn't work today. . . ."

"I'm tellin' you the truth, Mr. Ament. I didn't white-wash nothin' and . . ."

"Hobart is one of the most successful riverboat captains on the Mississippi. He wouldn't set folks up to be robbed."

"But there have been robberies," the boy persisted. "We've printed stories about 'em in the paper!"

Ament yawned and shook his head again. "Tell you what, Sam. I'll not fire you. Not just yet. And first thing Saturday morning . . ."

"That's two days away."

"First thing Saturday, I'll start looking into Captain Hobart. Poke around, ask some questions. Investigate like any good journalist would. There might be something in what you say, but . . ."

"But Captain Hobart will be gone then, especially if he knows we're askin' questions. Off down the river settin' more people up to be robbed in another town by someone like Junkyard Jim. We can't wait."

Boys are so impatient, I realized. But this one had reason. I found myself wishing Ament would take him more seriously.

"Sam, I *will* investigate this first before we print anything. And maybe we'll have a story by next Thursday or the one after. And maybe we won't." Then Ament shut the door.

The boy raised his fist to the wood again, but I nipped him in the side.

"Cat, I can't wait. If ol' Captain Hobart sees me in

town, he'll come after me again—and this time he'll kill me for certain. And I can't hide while Ament 'investigates' this. If ol' Captain Hobart catches wind of someone checkin' up on him, he'll kill me and then he'll be gone, never stoppin' in Hannibal again. I have to do somethin'."

I admired the boy's fervor. He had a purpose other than bothering cats. There was something almost noble about him. The way his arm was crooked beneath me left his fingers just beneath my chin. I moved my head and nipped at his thumb, not so hard as to draw blood, though. And I rubbed my jaw against his fingers.

Be a smart boy, I thought. *Look to yourself for the answer.*

The light from the stars and the light from the lamp inside the Ament place was enough. The boy could see his hands. They were dirty, from being dragged in the mud and from running along the walls in the cave. But there was more than dirt, there was a black settled in the whorls of his fingers. Ink from being Ament's cub.

"I set type," he told me.

Smart boy.

Then we were off again, down another alley and then turning on a street that paralleled the river. "What we're doin' ain't legal, breakin' into a place like this—even though I work here. But our crime ain't near so bad as what Hobart and Jim are guilty of. Ours is a good crime . . . if there's such a thing." He moved around to the back of a building and worked at the doorknob before it gave up and turned. "Lock doesn't hold none too good," he explained.

Inside, he finally set me down, and I watched as he lit a few lanterns. We were in a shop filled with cabinets and paper, big containers of ink, rollers, and a great contraption of metal larger than a bear. The boy continued to babble on, and I realized that in all my years boys had never talked *to* me, only *at* me as they were throwing things.

"I don't normally wet it down until Saturday, cat," he said, gesturing at the great contraption. "Turn it Sunday. See, we're a weekly, and the paper comes out on Thursday. That means one came out this mornin'. No wonder Ament was mad. I wasn't around to deliver it at dawn. 'Cept, I can't wait until next Thursday or the one after to tell my story. We're gonna print us up a special edition, cat. Tonight! And ol' Captain Hobart'll have the front page all to hisself. Gotta get the date right. August thirteenth, eighteen forty-eight."

I watched the boy work. "Only one page, cat, and I'll use the large type to take up space. Hope I can spell everythin' right." His fingers were plucking pieces of metal from racks—letters, he explained. Nearly all of these he arranged in rows, but he threw some bits away. "These're no good," he said. "Bent, worn, can't get a good print from 'em." He tossed them in a box. "Gotta throw the bad pieces away, into the hell matter." He paused. "I think ol' Captain Hobart and Junkman Jim belong in the hell matter, too." He smiled wide. "Jail is a hell matter box for bad people."

Despite being up so many hours, and frequently complaining about his sore head, he toiled without stop. Me? I slept off and on and wondered in between if the boy might think to feed me. I had, indeed, rescued him from the cave. I saved his life. And I had, by nipping his thumb, urged him to tell his tale to all of Hannibal now, rather than next Thursday. The boy owed me a meal.

It was dawn when the boy was finished pressing his one-sheet newspapers. He read the headline to me:

Respected Riverboat Captain Daniel Hobart
Mastermind Behind Scheme to Rob Passengers
Hannibal's Junkman Jim in Cahoots

"Not the best turn of phrase, cat," the boy told me. "But then I ain't had me a chance to write the news before. Good for a first effort, don't you think?"

I meowed my approval.

Later I clung to the buildings, watching him as he scurried from business to business to house to house, delivering his special edition and knocking on doors to wake up those still sleeping inside. He was careful to stay away from the river, not wanting to cross paths with Captain Hobart. And when he spotted Junkman Jim—fortunately Jim was looking the other way—the boy disappeared down an alley.

He did feed me well when he was finished, and he carried me up to a room above a drugstore, where both of us lay down on a small bed and slept the rest of the day away.

It was a week later, a fine Thursday morning, that Sam and I sat on the bank of the river, watching a steamer pass by. Captain Hobart and Junkman Jim were safely tucked away in a hell matter box—Hannibal's jail, and word was they were to be shipped down to St. Louis to begin a long sentence. More would be joining them, as Hobart had others like Junkman Jim working for him in several river towns in Missouri and Iowa.

Sam had delivered all the regular editions of the Hannibal *Courier*—that contained more detailed stories about Hobart and his gang—and was declared finished for the day. Ament hadn't fired him, rather he'd given the boy a modest raise and the title of assistant editor. Sam seemed pleased at this.

I was pleased, too.

For the first time in my long years, I had a home. Above a drugstore in the heart of Hannibal, a place at the foot of Sam's bed. For the rest of my days I was fed well and given saucers of milk, and I went to work with Sam on all the mornings my legs felt like carrying me.

I never cared much for boys.

Except for this one.

Two quotes that inspired this tale:

"The chairman's historical reminiscences of Gutenberg have caused me to fall into reminiscences, for I myself am something of an antiquity. All things change in the procession of years, and it may be that I am among strangers. It may be that the printer of today is not the printer of thirty-five years ago. I was no stranger to him. I knew him well. I built his fire for him in the winter mornings; I brought his water from the village pump; I swept out his office; I picked up his type from under his stand; and, if he were there to see, I put the good type in his case and the broken ones among the 'hell matter,' and if he wasn't there to see, I dumped it all with the 'pi' on the imposing-stone—for that was the furtive fashion of the cub, and I was a cub. I wetted down the paper Saturdays, I turned it Sundays—for this was a country weekly; I rolled, I washed the rollers, I washed the forms, I folded the papers, I carried them around at dawn Thursday mornings."

—*Samuel Clemens (Mark Twain) from his address at the Typothetae dinner commemorating the birthday of Benjamin Franklin, given at Delmonico's, January 18, 1886.*

"Of all God's creatures there is only one that cannot be made the slave of the leash. That one is the cat. If

man could be crossed with the cat it would improve
man, but it would deteriorate the cat."

—Mark Twain Notebook, 1894

About the Authors

While working on successful careers separately **Robert J. Randisi and Christine Matthews** have also managed to forge a second career each as a writing duo. They have written short stories and edited anthologies together, as well as penning the "Gil & Claire Hunt" novels *Murder Is the Deal of the Day* and *The Masks of Auntie Laveau*.

After starting out in science fiction and fantasy, **Lillian Stewart Carl** is now writing contemporary romantic suspense and mystery novels as well as mystery and fantasy stories. One novel is available in audio form. Several books and stories are available in electronic form from Fictionwise.com. She finds herself inventing her own genre, mystery/fantasy/romance with historical underpinnings. She especially enjoys the history of Scotland, where she's visited many times and where she's set more than a few works of fiction, including novels such as *Shadows In Scarlet* and *The Secret Portrait*. Lillian's website is at www.lillianstewartcarl.com.

Kristine Kathryn Rusch has won awards for her fiction in four different genres. She has published more than 70 books under various pen names. Under her own name in mystery, she is an Edgar finalist for her story, "Spinning," and has won the *Ellery Queen's Mystery Magazine* Readers Choice award. Her short mystery fiction can be found in the collection, *Little Miracles and Other Tales of Murder* from Five Star Publishing.

P. N. Elrod is the author of 20 novels and as many short stories. She's usually on another planet, but maintains citizenship in the state of Texas for tax purposes, and lives quite comfortably with her dogs, Sasha and Megan, and a full-size Dr. Who TARDIS she once built when she had too much time on her hands. (We'll gloss over the K-9 in her living room.) Her hair remains red nearly all the time, except when it's on fire because of a deadline. Everything else is subject to rewrite. Check out her website at www.vampwriter.com. The character of Escott is a major player in her Vampire Files mystery series. This story shows what trouble he gets into on a "normal" case!

A past president of Mystery Writers of America and winner of its Edgar award for best short story, **Edward D. Hoch** was honored in 2001 with MWA's Grand Master Award. He has been a guest of honor at the annual Bouchercon mystery convention, two-time winner of its Anthony Award, and 2001 recipient of its Lifetime Achievement Award. In 2000 he received The Eye, the life achievement award of the Private Eye Writers of America. Author of some 860 published stories as well as anthologies, collections and novels, Hoch resides with his wife Patricia in Rochester, NY.

John Helfers is a writer and editor currently living in Green Bay, Wisconsin. A graduate of the University of Wisconsin-Green Bay, his fiction appears in more than thirty anthologies and magazines. His first edited anthology, *Black Cats and Broken Mirrors*, was published by DAW Books in 1998 and has been followed by several more, including *Alien Abductions, Star Colonies, Warrior Fantastic, Knight Fantastic, The Mutant Files, Villains Victorious, Once*

Upon a Star, and *Space Stations.* His most recent nonfiction project was co-editing *The Valdemar Companion,* a guide to the fantasy world of Mercedes Lackey. Future projects include more anthologies as well as a novel in progress.

Brendan DuBois is the award-winning author of short stories and novels. His short fiction has appeared in *Playboy, Ellery Queen's Mystery Magazine, Alfred Hitchcock's Mystery Magazine, Mary Higgins Clark Mystery Magazine,* and numerous anthologies. He has twice received the Shamus Award from Private Eye Writers of America for his short stories and has been nominated three times for an Edgar Allan Poe Award by the Mystery Writers of America. He's also the author of the Lewis Cole mystery series—*Dead Sand, Black Tide, Shattered Shell,* and *Killer Waves.* He lives in New Hampshire with his wife Mona. His short stories have recently been collected in *Tales from the Dark Woods* by Five Star Publishing. Visit his website at www.BrendanDuBois.com.

Ed Gorman has garnered acclaim no matter what genre he writes in. Britain's *Million* magazine called him "one of the world's great storytellers." Reviewing his western work, the *Rocky Mountain News* said, "Quite simply, Ed Gorman is one of the best western writers of our time." A review in *The Magazine of Fantasy & Science Fiction* said, "Gorman is a skillful writer (who turns) the reader's expectations upside down, which is refreshing and disquieting." He has won several awards, most notably the Shamus and the Spur, and been nominated for the Edgar, Stoker, and the Golden Dagger. His work has appeared in such diverse magazines as *Redbook, Ellery Queen's Mystery Magazine,* and *Poetry Today.* He lives in Cedar Rapids, Iowa, with his wife, children's fiction author Carol Gorman.

Mat Coward is a British writer of short stories, novels, and sundry bespoke items. His critically acclaimed and popular novels *Up and Down* and *In and Out* were published by Five Star Publishing. His first children's novel was recently published in the UK, and a collection of his short crime fiction, *Do the World a Favour and Other Stories* was recently published by Five Star.

Gary A. Braunbeck has written numerous short stories in a variety of genres. His most recent collection, *Graveyard People: The Collected Cedar Hill Stories*, Vol. 1, will be released later this year from Earthling Publications.

Jean Rabe likes cats, but she isn't owned by any. Her husband is horribly allergic, and so they have two wonderful dogs and a miniature macaw, who frequently says, "Here kitty, kitty, kitty." She is the author of a dozen novels and more than two dozen short stories. She's also edited three anthologies and more magazine issues than she can easily count. In her spare time she plays games, visits museums, and pretends to garden.